簡明初級英文法

英文法

下

謝國平 編著

三民書局

國家圖書館出版品預行編目資料

簡明初級英文法／謝國平編著.－－初版九刷.－－
臺北市：三民，2011
　2冊：　　面；　　公分
　ISBN 978－957－14－1931－2　（上冊）
　ISBN 978－957－14－1932－9　（下冊）

　1.英國語言—文法

805.16/8255　　V. 2

© **簡明初級英文法（下）**

編著者　謝國平
發行人　劉振強
著作財　三民書局股份有限公司
產權人　臺北市復興北路386號
發行所　三民書局股份有限公司
　　　　地址／臺北市復興北路386號
　　　　電話／(02)25006600
　　　　郵撥／0009998－5
印刷所　三民書局股份有限公司
門市部　復北店／臺北市復興北路386號
　　　　重南店／臺北市重慶南路一段61號
初版一刷　1993年1月
初版九刷　2011年8月
編　號　S 800830
行政院新聞局登記證局版臺業字第○二○○號

ISBN　978－957－14－1932－9　（下冊：平裝）
http://www.sanmin.com.tw　三民網路書店

序

　　國民中學的英語教材近年來以溝通教學法爲編寫的基礎。在可見的未來時日裏，注重溝通的教學法將是國中英語教材的骨幹。雖然溝通教學法特別注重語意及語用的功能，但是，語意及語用是建構於文法的基礎上。如果文法不對，即使能溝通，充其量其英語只是洋涇浜英語。因此，雖然現行國中教科書上沒有「文法」這一欄，但其句型部分卻也是文法結構的介紹。

　　然而，編者總認爲，在學習英語初期雖然不必刻意強調文法教學，但基本的結構體認還是必需的。對文法的認識也應該循序且有系統地培養。基於這種理念，編者決定以《簡明現代英文法》爲基礎，選取適合國中程度的內容，精簡成一本國中學生適用的文法書，希望能配合國中的英語課本，增強學生對英語文法結構的了解，作爲進一步培養聽、說、讀、寫四技能的基礎。

　　本書編寫的原則，與《簡明現代英文法》無異——文字要簡易，資料要新，語用原理原則要說明，習題要足夠。然而要達成此四原則並使內容切合國中學生的程度與需要，實非易事。編寫過程中，雖盡力以過去多年輔導中學英語教學經驗作爲取材及設計習題的參考，但疏漏及不週延之處定難全免。尚祈使用本書的教師、學生以及所有讀者多予指正，是所至感。

謝國平　謹誌

臺北　師大英語系

八十一年五月

主要參考資料

Aronson, Trudy. *English Grammar Digest*. Englewood Cliffs, New Jersey: Prentice – Hall, Inc., 1984.

Jesperson, Otto. *A Modern English Grammar: On Historical Principle*. Vol.1 – Vol.7.

Marcellar, Frank. *Modern English: A Pratical Reference Guide*. Englewood Cliffs, New Jersey: Prentice – Hall, Inc., 1972.

Murphy, Raymond. *English Grammar in Use*. London: Cambridge University Press, 1985.

Quirk, Randolph, Sidney Greenbaum, Geoffrey Leech, and Jan Svartvik. *A Grammar of Contemporary English*. London: Longman, 1972.

Quirk, Randolph, Sidney Greenbaum, Geoffrey Leech, and Jan Svartvik. *A Comprehensive Grammar of the English Language*. London: Longman, 1985.

Swan, Michael. *Practical English Usage*. Oxford: Oxford University Press, 1980.

Swan, Michael. *Basic English Usage*. Oxford: Oxford University Press, 1984.

Thompson, A. J., & A. V. Martinet. *A Practical English Grammar*. 4 th edition, Hong Kong: Oxford University Press, 1986.

Wren, P. C. and H. Martin. *High School English Composition*. Bombay: K. & J. Cooper, 1962.

《簡明現代英文法》

簡明初級英文法(下)
目　次

序

主要參考書目

第十五章　冠詞

第十六章　形容詞

第十七章　副詞

第十八章　介詞

第十九章　不定詞

第二十章　分詞

第二十一章　動名詞

第二十二章　關係子句

第二十三章　連接詞與子句

第二十四章　條件句與假設句

第二十五章　引導詞 It 與 There

第二十六章　基本溝通功能的表達

第二十七章　直接引述與間接引述

第二十八章　連接兩句簡單句時語詞之省略

第十五章
冠詞

15.1. 冠詞的種類

　　冠詞(Article)為置於名詞前面的語詞，廣義地說，冠詞也是修飾語之一，對其後面的名詞加以限制。(例如指出該名詞有沒有特指)

　　冠詞分為「定冠詞」(definite article) *the*, 以及「不定冠詞」(indefinite article) *a*、*an* 兩種。

　　一般來說，冠詞的用法很複雜，而且中文裏並沒有與英文冠詞完全相同的詞類，中國學生學冠詞的用法時，困難特別多。然而，在一切冠詞使用法則說明之前，我們不妨先記住以下一項通則：「**可數單數普通名詞的前面一定要有冠詞**」。

　　因此，*Child is here.　*Book is mine.　*I want book. 是不合文法的句子。應說成 *The(A) child is here. The book is mine.* 及 *I want the(a) book.* 方可。

　　這個通則雖不能告訴我們如何使用冠詞，但至少能提供我們一個初步的警訊，減少犯錯誤的機會。

15.2.　定冠詞：the

定冠詞 *the* 有下列用法：

15.2.1.　定冠詞表示特指

定冠詞 *the* 置於名詞前面時，表示這名詞是有特定指稱，亦即是指說話者與聽者都知道的，或是在說話當時的場合中可以知道的人、地、事、物。也因此，*the* 稱爲「**定冠詞**」。例如：

　　the boy（指特定的一個男孩子）

　　the students（指特定的一群學生）

　　the book（指特定的一本書）

　　the books（指特定的一些書）

　　the honor（指特定的一項榮譽）

　　the 的特指用法可細分爲下列幾種：

⑴在說話當時的情況中可以辨認或知道的人、地、事、物名詞前，以 *the* 表示其特指。例如：

1. *The steak* smells good. 這牛排聞起來不錯。（在餐桌上說這句話，指的是桌上的那塊牛排）

2. *The boys* over there are my students. 在那邊的男孩子是我的學生。（聽者在說話當時可以看見的一群男孩子）

3. Have you fed *the dog*? 你餵了狗沒有？（在家中說這句話，指的是家人都知道的，家裏所養的那隻狗）

(2) *the* 用於說話者與聽者都有的一般共識，通常指比較大或廣泛的情況，也常表示一種獨一無二的人或事物(如一國只有一元首等)。例如：

　　the President 總統（指說話者與聽者所同屬的國家的元首）

　　the Pope 教宗（世界上只有一位天主教的教宗）

其他的例子如：

the North Pole 北極	*the* universe 宇宙
the South Pole 南極	*the* earth 地球
the sun 太陽	*the* moon 月亮
the sky 天空	*the* Church 教會

(3) *the* 用來指先前或上文所說過之人、地、事、物。這是 *the* 最常用的用法之一。例如：

1. Mary bought *a book* yesterday, but *the book* was stolen this morning. Mary 昨天買了一本書，但這本書今天早上給人偷了。

2. Tom bought *a radio* and *a TV set*, but he returned *the radio* to the shop. Tom 買了一部收音機和一部電視機，但他把收音機退回店裏。

另外，上文雖未提及，但從常理可以推斷的人、地或事、物，也用定冠詞 *the*。例如：

3. We attend *a wedding* yesterday. *The bride* was very young but *the bridegroom* was very old. 我們昨天參加了一個婚禮，新娘很年輕，新郎却很老。

上面例 3 只提到「婚禮」，但我們可推斷，婚禮中一定有新娘與新郎，所以用定冠詞 *the*。

⑷後面接修飾語(通常是片語或子句)的名詞，其前面常用 *the* 來表示特指。例如:

1. *the* boy over there 在那邊的那個男孩子(不是任何一個)

2. *the* bicycle (*that*) *my father gave me* 我父親給我的那輛腳踏車(不是任何一輛)

⑸在一些我們常去的場所、機關、或是一些交通、通訊方式的名詞前面，我們也常用 *the*。例如:

1. John goes to *the movie theater* every week. John 每星期都上電影院。

2. She likes to watch *the 7 o'clock news* on TV. 她喜歡看電視上的七點鐘新聞報告。

3. I'll talk to him over *the telephone*. 我會在電話裏跟他談一談。

其他的例子如: the radio(收音機)、the papers(報紙)、the bus(公共汽車)、the plane(飛機)、the mail(郵政，英式英語 "the post")、the train(火車)、the press(新聞界)等。

⑹邏輯上獨一的指稱常用定冠詞 *the*。這種用法最常見的是 the first '第一'、the last '最後'、the second '第二'、the next '第二個、下一個'、the same '相同的'、the only '唯一'、以及形容詞的最高級如 the best '最好的'、the worst '最壞的 '、the smallest '最小的'、the largest '最大的' 等。例如:

1. She is *the only girl* in our class. 她是我們班上唯一的女孩子。

2. Buddy and Mary have *the same interest*. Buddy 和 Mary 有相同的興趣

3. I want to take *the next bus.* 我想坐下一班公車。

(7)在介詞與表示身體部分的名詞之間，常用定冠詞 *the*。例如：

1. Edward hit me *on the head.* Edward 打我的頭。

2. Janet pulled her sister *by the hair.* Janet 拉她妹妹的頭髮。

3. He patted me *on the shoulder.* 他拍我的肩膀。

4. He kissed her *on the cheek.* 他吻她的臉頰。

15.2.2. 定冠詞表示泛指

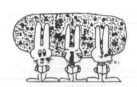

the 可以泛指人或事、物。

(1)與單數名詞連用時，可以單一個體代表全類／整體。例如：

1. He plays *the piano* well. 他彈鋼琴彈得很好. (泛指鋼琴這種樂器)

2. *The wheel* is one of the most important inventions in man's history. 輪子是人類歷史上最重要的發明之一。(泛指所有的輪子)

3. *The tiger* is a carnivorous animal. 老虎是食肉的動物。(泛指老虎這種動物)

(2)與表示國籍或民族的名詞連用時，可泛指該國或該民族的人。例如：

the Chinese 中國人

the Americans 美國人　等。

(3)「*the* ＋形容詞」可以泛指具有該形容詞特性的人，與複數動詞連用。
例如：

　　　the young 年輕人　　　　the blind 盲人

　　　the poor 窮人　　　　　　the rich 有錢人

　　　the old 老人　　　　　　　the elderly 年長者

　　　the brave 勇者　　　　　　the weak 弱者　等。

　　　The poor always *need* help. 窮人總是需要幫助的。

15.2.3. 定冠詞 the 與專有名詞

　　專有名詞原則上不帶冠詞，但有些專有名詞前面要加定冠詞 the。這些
名詞可分為以下幾類。

(1)**群島、山脈、湖泊等（複數形式的名詞）**。例如：

　　　the Philippines 菲律賓群島

　　　the Bahamas 巴哈馬群島

　　　the Alps 阿爾卑斯山脈

　　　the Rockies 洛磯山脈

　　　the Himalayas 喜馬拉雅山脈

　　　the Great Lakes 美國北方的五大湖

(2)**地理名詞**。例如：

　　河流：

　　　the Thames 泰晤士河

　　　the Yangtze River 揚子江（長江）

the Rhine 萊茵河

海洋:
the Atlantic Ocean 大西洋
the Pacific Ocean 太平洋
the Black Sea 黑海

運河:
the Suez Canal 蘇彝士運河
the Panama Canal 巴拿馬運河

其他地理名詞:
the Gulf of Mexico 墨西哥灣
the Cape of Good Hope 好望角
the Malay Peninsula 馬來半島
the Sahara Desert 撒哈拉沙漠
the Far East 遠東
the South Pole 南極
the North Pole 北極

(3)**公共機構、設施等**。例如:
the British Museum 大英博物館
the Library of Congress 美國國會圖書館
the White House 白宮
the Grand Hotel (飯店名)圓山大飯店
the Empire State Building 帝國大廈

⑷**船、飛機等名稱**。例如:

the Titanic 鐵達尼號郵輪

the Spirit of St. Louis 聖路易精神號(林白於 1927 年 5 月 2 日飛越大西洋所駕駛之飛機)

⑸**報章、雜誌等**。例如:

The New York Times 紐約時報

The United Daily News 聯合報

⑹**其他的專有名詞**。例如:

the Tang Dynasty 唐朝

the British Empire 大英帝國

the Rotary Club 扶輪社

the Y.M.C.A. 基督教青年會

the United States of America 美國

the United Nations 聯合國

the United Kingdom 聯合王國(英國)

15.3. 不定冠詞: a/an

不定冠詞有兩種形式, *an* 用於母音(發音)起始之名詞前面, *a* 則用於子音(發音)起首之名詞前面。*a/an* 只與單數可數名詞連用。

不定冠詞 *a/an* 主要用法有下列幾種:

(1) *a/an* 表示其後面之名詞並無特別指稱。因此，*a/an* 最常用於第一次提及的名詞前面。例如：

1. I bought *a book* yesterday. *The book* is interesting. 我昨天買了一本書，那本書很有趣。

2. I really want to see *a good movie.* 我眞的想看一場好電影。（哪一部電影則不知道、或未定）

3. He is *a good student.* 他是一個好學生。

(2) *a/an* 與 *one*

a/an 表示 '一'，因此 *one* 可以取代 *a/an*，但 *one* 的語氣要比 *a/an* 略爲強。例如：

He has two sons and *a daughter.*

He has two sons and *one daughter.* 他有兩個兒子和一個女兒。

但注意： 泛指的 *a/an* 不能用 *one* 來取代。例如：A cat is a domestic animal.（貓是家畜）一句中，*A* cat 不能說成 *One* cat。

(3) *a/an* 泛指的用法

a/an 可泛指全類中任何一份子。例如：

1. *A tiger* is a carnivorous animal. 老虎是肉食的動物。（泛指任一隻老虎）

2. *A sonnet* is a 14-line poem. 商籟詩是含有十四行的詩。（泛指任何一首 sonnet）

(4)專有名詞當普通名詞使用時，加不定冠詞 *a/an*，表示具有類似這個人的特性的人，或是名字如此的人。例如：

1. *a Shakespear* 一位像莎士比亞的作家

2. I used to know *a John Smith*. 我過去認識一位名叫 John Smith 的人。

⑸ *a* 與 *an* 可表示 "per" (每) 之意。例如:

1. I walk three miles *a* day. 我每天走三哩。

2. We are driving at 50 miles *an* hour. 我們正以每小時 50 哩的速度開車。

⑹ *a* 與 *an* 用法上之分別

　　a 與 *an* 用法上之分別是以發音爲依據, *an* 用於發音爲母音起首之字, *a* 用於發音爲子音開始之字。因此, 我們切勿受拼寫所影響。大多數情形下, 母音與子音並不易混淆。例如:

　　an *a*pple

　　an *o*range

　　an *i*nteresting story

　　an *e*xciting game

　　an *u*ninteresting lesson

　　a *b*oy

　　a *g*irl

　　a *s*ecretary 　　等等。

然而, 我們應注意以下幾點。

⒜首字母爲 *o*, 但發音爲 [w] 者, 用 *a*。例如:

　　a *one*-eyed cat 獨眼的貓

　　a *one*-sided story 片面的說法

　　a *one*-way street 單行道

a one-man boat 單人操作的小艇

(b)首字母為 *u*、*eu*、*ew* 但發音為 [j] 者，用 *a*。例如：

*a u*niversity 大學

*a E*uropean 歐洲人

*a ew*e 母羊

*a u*seful tool 有用的工具

*a u*sed car 舊車，二手車

(c)首字母為不發音的 *h*，後接母音者，用 *an*。例如：

*an h*our 一小時

*an h*eir 繼承人

*an h*onest man 誠實的人

(d)發音以母音為起字的數字、字母、略語等，用 *an*。例如：

an 8 一個 8 字

an h 一個 h 字

an n 一個 n 字

an f 一個 f 字

an M.A. degree 一個碩士學位

(這些字的發音是：8 [et]、h[etʃ]、n[ɛn]、f[ɛf]、M.A.[`ɛm`e])

15.4.　以下情形不用冠詞

一般說來，大多數的專有名詞及不可數名詞前面，不用冠詞。除此之外，

下列情形也**不用冠詞**。

⑴複數名詞及單數不可數名詞用於泛指時, 不用冠詞。例如:

1. *Tigers* are carnivorous animals. 老虎是肉食動物。
2. *Cigarettes* are bad for our health. 香烟有害我們的健康。
3. *Oil* is lighter than *water*. 油比水輕。

⑵*school*、*church*、*town*、*hospital*、*bed*、*class* 等詞語前面, 特別表示這些語詞所含之活動或功能, 而不表示其場所本身時, 不用冠詞。例如:

1. He goes to *school* every day. 他每天上學。
2. He goes to *church* every Sunday. 他每星期天都上敎堂。
3. She is still in *bed*. 她還在睡。

試比較:

4. He will wait for us at the gate of *the school*. 他會在那個學校的大門口等我們。(the school 指的是 '場所', 並非 '上學' 這種 '活動'。)
5. She lay down on *the bed*. 她躺在那張床上。(the bed 指的是 '場所', 而非 '睡覺' 這種 '活動' 或 '功能'。)

⑶在 *by* 後面, 表示交通或通訊方式的名詞前面, 不用冠詞。例如:

交通:

by bicycle (騎)單車
by bus (坐)公共汽車
by car (坐)汽車
by boat (坐)船

by train （乘）火車

by plane （坐）飛機　等。

通訊:

by radio （以/用）無線電廣播

by telegram （以/用）電報

by telephone （以/用）電話

by mail （美式英語）（以/用）郵寄

by post （英式英語）（以/用）郵寄

1. We'll go *by plane*. 我們會坐飛機去。

2. I will send you the book *by airmail*. 我會把這本書用航空郵寄給你。

(4)在介詞 *at*、*by*、*after* 及 *before* 後面, 表示一天當中某個時間的名詞前面, 不用冠詞。例如:

at dawn/at daybreak　黎明、破曉

at sunrise　日出

at sunset　日落

at noon　中午

at night　晚上

at midnight　半夜

by day　日間

by night　夜間

before dawn　黎明以前

after dark　天黑以後

(*by*) *day and night*　日夜　等。

1. He does his homework *at night*. 他晚上做功課。

2. She never goes to bed *before midnight*. 半夜以前她從不睡覺。

(5)表示季節的名詞前面，通常可以不用冠詞。例如：

1. We often go swimming *in* (*the*) *summer*. 夏天我們常去游泳。

2. She never goes skiing *in* (*the*) *winter*. 她冬天從不去滑雪。

注意：表示特定的某一個季節時，要用 *the*。例如：

　　the spring of 1985 1985 年的春天

　　the fall/autumn of last year 去年的秋天

(6)表示每天的三餐的名詞前，通常也不用冠詞。例如：

1. Will you stay *for dinner*? 你會留下來吃晚飯嗎？

2. We discussed our plans *at breakfast* this morning. 今天早上我們吃早餐時討論我們的計劃。

其他的例子如：after lunch '午飯後'、before supper '晚飯前'、at dinner/lunch/tea '在(吃)晚飯/午飯/下午茶時' 等等。

注意：指特定的某一次用餐時，要用 the。例如：

3. *The lunch* we had at that new restaurant this afternoon was quite good. 今天下午我們在那家新開的餐館吃的那頓午飯相當不錯。

(7)疾病名稱前面通常也不用冠詞。例如：diabetes '糖尿病'、pneumonia '肺炎'、measles '麻疹'、influenza/flu '流行性感冒'、cancer '癌'、mumps '腮腺炎、乍腮'、chicken pox '水痘' 等。

⑻在一些對稱結構的成語中，冠詞常省略不用。例如：

　　arm in arm 臂挽臂

　　hand in hand 手牽手

　　face to face 面對面

　　back to back 背對(靠)背

　　side by side 相鄰(並肩)

　　shoulder to shoulder 肩並肩

　　day by day, day after day 日復一日

　　eye for eye 以牙還牙

　　word by word, word for word 逐字

　　husband and wife 夫妻

　　father and son 父子

　　from left to right 從左到右

　　from beginning to end 從頭到尾　等。

這些片語中，名詞重複者通常具有副詞的功能。例如：

　　We must do this ***step by step***. 我們必須逐步地做這事。

⑼很多帶介詞的片/成語中，其名詞前面不用冠詞。除前面已提到的 at home、in bed、by car、at dawn 等以外。其他的例子如：

　　on foot 步行

　　in turn 依次

　　out of step 亂了步伐

　　on top of ...　在…之上

　　on fire 著火、燃燒著

　　in fact 事實上　等。

類似這些片語的用語很多，初學者只能多看多用、多查字典，透過實際例句來學習並記憶這些片語/成語。

《習題19》

(A)下列空格中，請按文法需要，填入冠詞 *a, an* 或 *the*。如不需冠詞，則留空不填。

例：John wants to buy ＿＿＿*a*＿＿＿ radio.

1. I gave Priscilla ＿＿＿＿ expensive watch as her ＿＿＿＿ birthday present.

2. I bought ＿＿＿＿ book yesterday. ＿＿＿＿ book is very interesting.

3. Spain (西班牙) is ＿＿＿＿ European country.

4. We need ＿＿＿＿ new English teacher because our English teacher has resigned (辭職).

5. She will be back in ＿＿＿＿ hour.

6. I want to talk to ＿＿＿＿ man over there.

7. Jane was driving at ＿＿＿＿ speed of 50 miles ＿＿＿＿ hour.

8. He left ＿＿＿＿ Taiwan for ＿＿＿＿ United States last week.

9. Both of us wanted to watch ＿＿＿＿ 7:30 news on TV.

10. Did you read ＿＿＿＿ note on the desk?

(B)填入適當的冠詞。如不需冠詞時，則留空不填。

1. People need ＿＿＿＿ water and ＿＿＿＿ food.

2. I want ＿＿＿＿ piece of bread.

3. He was infected (被感染) with ＿＿＿＿ measles.

4. She is studying ＿＿＿＿ Japanese.

5. I never listen to ＿＿＿＿ punk (龐克) music.

6. She likes _____ bread and butter.

7. Many of _____ students in our class work very hard.

8. He doesn't like _____ meat.

9. Horace has written _____ excellent(極好的) composition(作文).

10. He works very hard because he wants to earn enough _____ money
    to send his _____ son to _____ college.

11. I want you to go to _____ bed at 10:00 p.m..

12. Does it rain a lot in _____ New York?

13. Janet gets up early in _____ morning.

14. The new book looks like _____ old one.

15. I don't like _____ bread.

(C)以下各句中，在需要的地方加上適當的冠詞。

　　例：I found cat.

　　　　I found _____*a*_____ cat.

1. Our teacher wrote three words on blackboard yesterday.

2. We rent(租) this room by month.

3. She is best student in our class.

4. Tom hit her on nose.

5. Jane is looking at sky.

6. John was born in small town near Shanghai(上海).

7. We do not have ray of hope.

8. Alice went to British Museum last week.

(D)在以下空格中填入適當的冠詞，如不需冠詞，則留空不填。

1. Tracy is _____ friend of mine.

2. She can play _____ piano very well.

3. I bought the meat by _____ pound.

4. My uncle teaches _____ violin(小提琴) at _____ private school (私立學校).

5. We will have no English classes for _____ next two days.

6. She took me by _____ hand.

7. He will be _____ first one to finish answering all _____ questions in _____ test.

8. He will go there by _____ ship.

9. _____ Pacific Ocean is _____ largest ocean in _____ world.

10. Mr. Lee is _____ English teacher. He has written _____ book on English grammar(文法).

11. _____ sun is like _____ great ball of _____ fire.(太陽像個大火球。)

12. Let's open our books and read _____ third lesson.

第十六章
形容詞

16.1. 形容詞的特徵

「形容詞」(Adjective)是修飾名詞或代名詞的語詞。除了這種最廣義的定義以外，形容詞通常還有以下四種文法上的特性：

(A)形容詞可置於名詞之前，修飾名詞。例如：

　　an **old** man 一位老人

　　a **naughty** boy 一個頑皮的男孩

注意：形容詞置於冠詞後面。

(B)形容詞可置於述語中，作主詞補語或受詞補語。例如：

The boy is **tired.** (主詞補語)這男孩子累了。

We thought him **ugly.** (受詞補語) 我們認為他很醜。

(C)大多數形容詞前面可以用「**強調副詞**」very 來修飾。例如：

very **good** 十分好, very **big** 十分大。

(D)形容詞可以有「**比較級**」(comparative degree)以及「**最高級**」(superlative degree)。例如:

happier 更快樂	happiest 最快樂
faster 比較快	fastest 最快
more beautiful 比較美麗	most beautiful 最美麗

當然, 並不是所有的形容詞上述四種特性全部都具備。例如有些形容詞只可置於述語中, 而不能置於名詞前面的, 我們可以說 The boy is *asleep.* (這男孩睡著了), 但却不可以說*the *asleep* boy。然而, 這四種文法上的特性, 的確也是形容詞在文法上的標誌, 能幫助我們對形容詞的用法有所了解。

16.2. 形容詞的文法功能

⑴屬性修飾與述語修飾

形容詞置於被修飾的名詞前面時, 稱為「**屬性形容詞**」(attributive adjectives), 亦即 16.1. 所舉的特性(A)。例如:

a *small* room 一個小房間

a *big* chair 一張大椅子

popular music 流行音樂

nice people 好人

形容詞如置於述語中, 作主詞跟受詞的補語時, 稱為「**述語形容詞**」(predicative adjectives), 亦即 16.1. 所舉的特性(B)。例如:

1. The boy is *happy.* (主詞補語) 這男孩子很快樂。

2. She seems *busy.* (主詞補語) 她似乎很忙碌。

3. We thought him *crazy.* (受詞補語) 我們以為他瘋了。

4. She made me *happy*. (受詞補語) 她使我快樂。

大多數的形容詞都可置於屬性修飾的位置, 很多形容詞同時可以用於屬性修飾以及述語修飾兩種位置。但是, 有些形容詞則只能用於這兩種位置中之一。

⑵只能用於屬性修飾位置的形容詞

⒜某些強調的形容詞

這些形容詞都是加強語氣的形容詞, 而且, 通常這些形容詞在語意上並不直接修飾名詞所指的人或物。例如:

1. an *old* friend 老朋友

2. a *complete* stranger 完全陌生的人

3. a *clear* victory 完全的勝利

例句1中的 old 並非以其本義「年老」之意來修飾 friend 一字。「老朋友」是指「友誼」本身的「久」而不是朋友的年歲「老」。因此, 國中學生之間, 有些可能是小學就認識的「老朋友」, 但是國中學生年紀都不能算老。

例句2中的 complete 是指「陌生」的程度, 因此我們翻譯為「完全陌生的人」, 而不能翻成「*完全的陌生人」。

例3的 clear 也是指勝利的程度, 是完全的。因此我們也不能以 clear 的本義「清楚」來翻譯。

當然, 如果這些形容詞並不是以強調形容詞使用, 是可以有述語修飾的用法的。例如: The man is very old. 那個男人很老。

⒝限制形容詞

有些形容詞對其修飾的名詞的指稱加以限制, 這類「限制形容詞」通常也只能用在屬性修飾位置。例如:

1. a *certain* student 某個學生

2. the *main* reason 主要的原因

3. the *same* teacher 同一位老師

4. the *only* classroom 唯一的教室

這些形容詞, 都對其後的名詞所指的人或物加以限制, 也不用於述語修飾位置。因此, 我們不可以說*The reason is main, *The classroom is only 等。

(3)只能用於述語修飾位置上的形容詞

(A)如形容詞本身是個詞組(或稱片語), 而詞組中的形容詞有其他語詞修飾(如 afraid *of him,* able *to win* 等), 這種形容詞詞組只能用於述語修飾位置。例如:

1. John is *afraid of her.* John 怕她。

2. I am *fond of him.* 我喜歡他。

3. We are *happy about the result.* 我們對這結果覺得高興。

(B)很多以字首「a-」開始的形容詞, 只用於述語修飾位置。例如:

1. She is *asleep.* 她睡著了。(她是睡著的)

2. The patient is still *alive.* 病人還是活著的。

3. The man is *alone.* 這男人是單獨的。

4. The two sisters are very much *alike.* 這兩姊妹十分相像。

(4)置於被修飾名詞後面的形容詞

形容詞如修飾以-*body, -one, -thing, -where* 結尾的複合詞(如 someone, something, anything)時, 置於這些複合詞之後。例如:

1. This is *something useful.* 這是有用的東西。(不能說*This is useful something.)

2. Do you see *anything wrong*? 你看見有什麼不對勁嗎?(不能說*Do you see wrong anything?)

3. Shall we go *somewhere* quiet? 我們到一個安靜的地方去好嗎?(不能說*Shall we go quiet somewhere?)

⑸形容詞當作名詞使用

形容詞置於 the 後面可使這形容詞具有名詞的功能。這種用法可分為三種:

⒜「*the*＋可修飾人的形容詞」可泛指具有該形容詞的特質的人。例如:
the young 泛指年輕的人, *the poor* 泛指窮人。注意: 動詞要用複數。

　　The poor need our help. 窮人需要我們的幫助。

⒝「*the*＋表示國家的形容詞」可泛指該國的人。這類國籍形容詞大多限於*-ch* 及*-sh* 結尾的字。例如:

　　the British 英國人
　　the French 法國人

⒞「*the*＋形容詞」可指抽象的事物, 尤其是當形容詞為最高級形式時。例如:

1. *The best* is yet to come. 最好的還未來到。
2. *The unknown* is always frightening. 未知(之事/之世界)總是使人害怕的。

其他的例子如 the last '最後的(事物)'、the latest '最近的/最新的(事物)'、the unreal '不真實的(事物)' 等等。

16.3. 形容詞的比較

16.3.1. 比較式的形式

對大多數形容詞而言，其語意都可分程度與等級的。例如：'高'、'比較高'、'最高' 等。在文法上，**形容詞的比較**（comparison of adjectives）可分爲「**原級**」（positive degree，如 small '小'），「**比較級**」（comparative degree，如 smaller '比較小'），以及「**最高級**」（superlative degree，如 smallest '最小'）。

原級的字形不變，比較級與最高級有兩種方式，其中之一是在原級後加-er 及-est 字尾，另一方式是在原級之前加 more 及 most。大多數的形容詞的比較都是依照這種規則的方式構成。除此以外，有一些形容詞的比較形式是以不規則的變化構成。以下我們列出並說明形容詞比較形式構成應注意的一些事項。

⑴**何時用詞尾*-er/-est*，何時用 *more/most*？**

一般說來，這種選擇大多取決於形容詞本身的長度。

(A)**單音節的字通常用詞尾-er、-est。例如：**

原級		比較級	最高級
tall	高	taller	tallest
small	小	smaller	smallest
low	低	lower	lowest

cold	冷	colder	coldest

但請**注意**：real '眞實'、right '正確'、wrong '錯誤'、like '相似、像' 等字用 more/most。例如：He is **more like** his father. '他更像他父親'。

(B)雙音節的字大多數用 more/most，但有些雙音節的字，特別是字尾是 *-y*、*-ow*、*-le*、*-er*、*-ure* 的形容詞，也可以用-er、-est 來構成比較級及最高級。例如：

原級		比較級	最高級
early	早	earlier	earliest
easy	容易	easier	easiest
funny	有趣、可笑	funnier	funniest
happy	快樂	happier	happiest
narrow	窄	narrower	narrowest
simple	簡單	simpler	simplest
clever	聰明	cleverer	cleverest
mature	成熟	maturer	maturest

注意：(a)以上這些形容詞都可以用 more/most 來形成比較級及最高級。

(b)雙音節字如 common '普通'、polite '有禮貌'、handsome '英俊' 等雖然可以加-er/-est，但現代用法比較傾向用 more 及 most。

(C)三音節及更長的形容詞只能用 more/most。例如：

原級		比較級	最高級
beautiful	美麗的	more beautiful	most beautiful

capable	有能力的	more capable	most capable
wonderful	奇妙的	more wonderful	most wonderful

注意：含 un-字首的形容詞例外，除用 more/most 以外，也可用-er/-est。例如：unhappy '不快樂'，more unhappy/unhappier, most un-happy/unhappiest。

(D)分詞形式的形容詞用 more/most。例如：

原級		比較級	最高級
interesting	有趣的	more interesting	most interesting
exciting	使人興奮的	more exciting	most exciting
confused	(受)困擾的	more confused	most confused
satisfied	滿意的	more satisfied	most satisfied

綜合而言，在當代英語中，除單音節字以外，形容詞的比較級及最高級多趨向使用 more/most 來構成。

(2)加詞尾-er/-est 時，在拼寫上應注意的事項。

形容詞加-er/-est 時，拼寫上與動詞加-ing, -s, 及-ed 詞尾時相似。

(A)如單音節形容詞字尾為單子音，其前面只有一個母音(唸短音)，亦即是 CVC 音節形態時，字根之最後子音要重覆。例如：

原級		比較級	最高級
big	大	bigger	biggest
fat	胖	fatter	fattest
sad	悲傷	sadder	saddest
thin	瘦	thinner	thinnest

hot	熱	hotter	hottest

(B)原級字尾為 y 時，y 改為 i 再加-er/-est。例如：

原級		比較級	最高級
early	早	earlier	earliest
happy	快樂	happier	happiest
healthy	健康	healthier	healthiest

(C)原字結尾為不發音的字母 e 時，刪除 e 再加-er/-est(亦即只須加上 r/st)。例如：

原級		比較級	最高級
late	遲	later	latest
brave	勇敢	braver	bravest
free	自由	freer	freest

(3)加詞尾 *-er/-est* 時，發音上應注意事項

(A)雙音節形容詞如第二音節含音節化 [l̩](即 syllabic [l̩])，加-er/-est 時，第二音節刪略不唸。例如：

　simple 簡單 [`sɪmpl̩]　simpler[`sɪmplɚ]　simplest[`sɪmplɪst]
　noble 高貴 [`nobl̩]　nobler[`noblɚ]　noblest[`noblɪst]
因此，加了-er/-est 後，仍為兩個音節。

(B)字尾為 ng(發音為 [ŋ])之形容詞，加-er/-est 後，在 [ŋ] 後加 [g]。例如：

　long　長 [lɔŋ]　　longer [`lɔŋgɚ]　longest [`lɔŋgɪst]
　strong 強壯 [strɔŋ]　stronger [`strɔŋgɚ] strongest[`strɔŋgɪst]

young　年輕的　[jʌŋ]　　younger [ˋjʌŋɡɚ]　youngest [ˋjʌŋɡɪst]

⑷不規則比較級及最高級

⒜有少數形容詞比較級及最高級與原式之字根不同。例如：

原級		比較級	最高級
good	好	better	best
well	好、健康	better	best
bad	壞、不好	worse	worst
much	多(量)	more	most
many	多(數)	more	most
little	少	less	least
far	遠	{ farther / further	{ farthest / furthest
old	老、年長	{ older / elder	{ oldest / eldest

⒝ older/oldest 與 elder/eldest

old/oldest 指年齡較老/最老，以及較舊/最舊之意。elder/eldest 則指家庭中年紀較大/最大。例如：

　　1. She is my **elder** sister. 她是我姊姊。

　　2. She is **older** than me (I). 她年紀比我大。

這種區別在英式英語中很常用，但在美式英語中，則常可用 older/oldest 來取代 elder/eldest。

⒞有些形容詞語意上不易分等級，因此沒有比較形式。例如：utter '完全'、only '唯一'、unique '獨一、唯一'、infinite '無限'、yearly '每年的'

等。

16.4.　比較句式

比較句式的結構有下列幾種：

⑴同等程度的比較

同等程度比較的句式：**as＋原級＋as**

1. Mrs. Li is ***as clever as*** Mrs. Wang. 李太太跟王太太一樣的聰明。

2. He is ***as tall as*** his grandfather. 他跟他祖父一樣高。

⑵不同程度的比較

(A)較優的比較用以下句式：**比較級＋*than***

1. He is ***taller than*** his elder brother. 他比他哥哥高。

2. This pencil is ***longer than*** that one. 這枝鉛筆比那枝長。

3. He is ***older than*** Mr. Chang. 他比張先生年紀大。

4. I read ***more*** books ***than*** you (do). 我看的書比你多。

5. She seems ***more confused than*** you (do). 她似乎比你更覺困擾。

(B)較劣的比較用以下句式：$\begin{cases} not\ so/as＋原級＋as \\ less＋比較級＋than \end{cases}$

1. This book is ***less expensive than*** that one. 這本書不及那本書貴。

2. This book is *not so* (*as*) *expensive as* that one. 這本書不及那本書貴。

3. He is *less nervous than* Mr. Wang. 他不及王先生緊張。

4. He is *not so* (*as*) *nervous as* Mr.Wang.他不及王先生緊張。

⑶三個或三個以上的人或事物的比較

三個或三個以上的比較用以下句式： $\begin{cases} the+最高級+of(人或事物) \\ the+最高級+in(地方) \end{cases}$

1. John is *the tallest* boy *in our class.* John 是我們班上最高的男生。

2. He is *the youngest* (one) *of the three boys.* 他是那三個男孩中年紀最小的一個。

3. She is *the cleverest of all my students.* 她是我所有學生中最聰明的一位。

4. Taipei is *the biggest* city *in Taiwan.* 臺北市是臺灣最大的城市。

⑷表示漸增或漸減用以下句式：比較級＋*and*＋比較級

1. The weather is getting *warmer and warmer.* 天氣愈來愈暖和。

2. She become *more and more nervous.* 她變得愈來愈緊張。

⑸對稱的比較用以下句式：*the*＋比較級…，*the*＋比較級…

1. *The older* he grows, *the wiser* he becomes. 他愈老愈有智慧。

2. A: Do you like a big apartment?　你喜歡大的公寓嗎?

B: Yes, *the bigger the better.* 是的，愈大愈好。

3. The *more diligent* you are, the *better grades* you will get in the exam. 你愈是勤勉，考試就會得到愈高的分數。

(6)倍數的比較用以下句式：倍數詞＋*as*＋原級＋*as*

1. I have *twice as many books as he.* 我的書比他的多上兩倍。

2. This classroom is *three times as big as* that one. 這間敎室比那間大三倍。

16.5. 比較句式中應注意的事項

⑴在類似以下的比較句中，*than* 後面的名詞可以用主格(正式用法)或用受格(非正式/口語)。例如：

正式：He is younger than *I am.* 他比我年輕。

正式：He is younger than *I.*

口語/非正式：He is younger than *me.*

⑵有些形容詞的比較級後面用 *to* 而不用 *than*。例如：He thinks he is *superior to* us. 他以爲他比我們優越。

類似的字不多，多屬外來字，如 inferior '劣於'、senior '長於'、junior '幼於'、anterior '前於/早於'、posterior '後於'、prior '前於/早於' 等。

⑶雙重比較是不合文法的。例如：

1.*He is *more stronger* than I (me). 他比我強壯。

正確的說法應該是：

2. He is **stronger** than I (me). 他比我強壯。

如果眞的要強調比較級形容詞時，可以用 much/far。例如：

3. He is **much** (**far**) **stronger** than I(me). 他比我強壯很多。

16.6. 形容詞的順序

如在屬性修飾的位置上(亦即在名詞之前)，有兩個或兩個以上的形容詞修飾同一名詞時，這些形容詞通常會有一個常用的順序。例如 a little brown dog '一隻棕色的小狗'、a beautiful new doll '一個美麗的新洋娃娃' 等。

形容詞的順序大致可綜合如下表：

冠詞、不定代名詞、指示代名詞等	數　　詞	一般性質	外在形態	國籍、宗教以及一些-al,-ic(al)結尾的形容詞	名詞或V-ing形式	名　　詞
a,an the this that some all every 等	one two seven first second third 等	beautiful interest- ing clever useful handsome good 等	big little long small old young new hot red 等	Chinese Italian Catholic commercial electronic electrical 等	silk cotton college fishing jet copying 等	girl student car machine district plane house 等

注意：(a)冠詞、不定代名詞等的順序是：**表分詞＞冠詞＞** $\left.\begin{array}{l}\textbf{指示詞}\\\textbf{所有格}\end{array}\right\}$**＞不**

定形容詞

例如：
half the students. 半數的學生
all those boys. 所有那些男孩子

(b)數詞的順序是：**序數＞基數**

例如：*the first two* lessons 前面的兩課

(c)外在形態形容詞的順序是：**大小＞外形＞年齡＞溫度＞顏色**

例如：*a little red* car 一部紅色小車子

a tall young girl 一個高的年輕女孩子

當然，上表所列的順序，並非一成不變的，有時候也可略有不同。但一般說來，表中及注意事項(a)至(c)的順序是比較常用的。其他例子如：

1. *a useful new electronic* computer 一部有用的新電子計算機
2. *that clever Catholic* student 那位聰明的信天主教的學生
3. *a beautiful silk* dress 一件美麗的絲質洋裝

《習題 20》

(A)將下列各句後面所提示的形容詞置於正確的位置上。並以箭號指出被修飾的語詞。

例：a. I have a hat. (new)

I have a *new* hat.

b. Nothing has happened. (new)

Nothing *new* has happened.

1. He needs some eggs. (fresh)

2. Miss Wang has met someone. (nice)

3. There were a few apples. (big)

4. She has a voice. (sweet)

5. Everything in the house was stolen. (valuable)

6. Can you see anything in this lesson? (wrong)

7. Do you want something? (sweet)

8. We had a few days last week. (sunny)

9. He gave me three stamps. (Italian)

10. Do you see anything in the room? (unusual)

(B)將下列句子的形容詞從屬性修飾位置改爲述語修飾位置，或是從述語修飾位置改
　　成屬性修飾位置。

　　例： a. The book is good.

　　　　　　It is a good book.

　　　　　 b. They are good books.

　　　　　　The books are good.

1. The story was interesting.

2. She is a clever girl.

3. It is a healthy baby.

4. The question is difficult.

5. They are good teachers.

6. The man is busy.

7. It is an exciting game.

8. The idea is good.

(C)以下列各形容詞造句。如形容詞可用於屬性及述語兩種修飾位置，則造兩句；如只
　　能置於述語修飾位置，則造一句。

例：a. red

　　The dress is *red*.

　　It is a *red* dress.

　　b. alone

　　　She is *alone*.

1. nice

2. interesting

3. alike

4. asleep

5. cold

6. happy

7. kind

8. afraid

9. simple

10. expensive

(D)把下列各句括號中的修飾語依正確的順序排好。

　　例：He is (good, a, old) man.

　　　He is a good old man.

1. He always talks about (old, good, the) days.

2. I just bought (expensive, an) book.

3. I will give her (nice, a, birthday) present.

4. Father gave me (gold, a, beautiful) watch.

5. She is (kind, the, little) girl that I told you about.

(E)把下列形容詞的比較級及最高級寫出。注意某些字的拼寫法。

　　例：big *bigger biggest*

	比較級	最高級
1. sweet	_____	_____
2. fine	_____	_____
3. cold	_____	_____
4. hot	_____	_____
5. happy	_____	_____
6. little	_____	_____
7. small	_____	_____
8. excited	_____	_____
9. beautiful	_____	_____
10. late	_____	_____
11. early	_____	_____
12. heavy	_____	_____
13. fat	_____	_____
14. thin	_____	_____
15. bad	_____	_____
16. dark	_____	_____
17. simple	_____	_____
18. cheap	_____	_____
19. expensive	_____	_____
20. serious	_____	_____

(F)以「as＋原級形容詞＋as」來表示程度相等的比較。

例： He is tall. ⎫
　　 She is tall. ⎭ → He is *as tall as* she.

1. Mr. Wang is kind. ⎫
　 Mr. Li is kind. ⎭ →

2. She is pretty. ⎱
   Mary is pretty. ⎰ →

3. This story is interesting. ⎱
   That story is interesting. ⎰ →

4. Tom seemed nervous. ⎱
   Larry seemed nervous. ⎰ →

5. He becomes confused. ⎱
   Mr. Chang becomes confused. ⎰ →

(G)以「形容詞比較級＋*than*」及「*not so*＋形容詞＋*as*」來合併以下各句子。

　　例： He is tall. ⎱ → He is *taller than* she(her).
　　　　 She is not tall. ⎰ → She is *not so tall as* he.

1. Tom is old. ⎱
   Peter is not old. ⎰ →

2. This building is old. ⎱
   That building is not old. ⎰ →

3. Alice was nervous. ⎱
   Mary was not nervous. ⎰ →

4. Jack is satisfied. ⎱
   Larry is not satisfied. ⎰ →

5. My method is good. ⎱
   Your method is not good. ⎰ →

(H)以「*less*＋形容詞＋*than*」及「*not so*＋形容詞＋*as*」來合併以下句子。

　　例： She is clever. ⎱ → He is *less clever than* she (her).
　　　　 He is not clever. ⎰ → He is *not as clever as* she.

1. Tom is friendly.
   Larry is not friendly. } →

2. Alice's story is exciting.
   Betty's story is not exciting. } →

3. Edward is smart.
   Steve is not smart. } →

4. Frank is dilligent.
   Dick is not dilligent. } →

5. Nancy is efficient (有效率).
   Cindy is not efficient. } →

第十七章
副詞

17.1. 副詞的簡介

簡單地說，**副詞**（Adverb）是修飾動詞、形容詞或另一副詞的語詞。例如：

　　1. He runs *fast.* 他跑得快。（修飾動詞）

　　2. She is *very* happy. 她很快樂。（修飾形容詞）

　　3. She sings *extremely* well. 她唱得好極了。（修飾副詞）

比較廣義的看，副詞也包括具有以上功能的片語。例如：

　　4. He left *in a hurry.* 他匆忙地離開了。

　　5. He came *this morning.* 他今天早上來。

至於具有副詞功能的子句（如 He saw me *when I was in New York.*），我們在以下第二十二章「**連接詞與子句**」一章中再詳細討論。本章所指的副詞，是指類似例句 1.至 5.中斜體的單字及片語。

17.2. 副詞的種類與位置

副詞可以分為以下六種：

狀態副詞　（adverbs of manner）
地方副詞　（adverbs of place）
時間副詞　（adverbs of time）
頻率副詞　（adverbs of frequency，又稱為「**頻度副詞**」）
程度副詞　（adverbs of degree，又稱為「**強調詞**」(intensifier)）
句副詞　　（sentence adverbs）

　　副詞在句子中能出現的位置比形容詞來得自由。同一個副詞有時候可置於不同的位置。大致上，最廣泛的通則是：修飾動詞的副詞常置於句末；修飾形容詞或副詞的副詞(如程度副詞)置於被修飾的字之前；修飾全句的副詞常置於句首。

17.2.1. 狀態副詞

　　狀態副詞表示動作的狀態，通常置於句末位置。例如：

1. She sings **beautifully**. 她唱歌唱得很甜美。
2. I can type **fast**. 我打字可以打得很快。
3. He came **happily**. 他高高興興地來了。
4. I wrote the letter **with care**(＝carefully). 我小心地寫了這封信。

　　-ly 結尾的副詞有時候也可以置於動詞前面(句中位置)。這種位置常用於「**主詞＋動詞＋受詞**」的句型中，尤其是受詞後面帶有較長的片語或子句修

飾語時，副詞更要置於動詞前面。例如：

> 5. She *carefully* washed the new dishes (that) her mother bought yesterday. 她小心地洗了那些她媽媽昨天買回來的新盤子。

另外，狀態副詞可以作 how 起首的 wh-問句的回應。例如：

> 6. A: *How* does she sing?
>   B: She sings *beautifully*.(或簡單地說 *Beautifully*.)
> 7. A: *How* did he come?
>   B: He came *happily*.(或簡單地說 *Happily*)

17.2.2. 地方副詞

地方副詞表示動作之處所，通常置於句末。例如：

> 1. He went *upstairs*. 他到樓上去。
> 2. She stayed *at home*. 她留在家裏。
> 3. I sent him *away*. 我叫他走開。
> 4. She sat *there*. 她坐在那兒。
> 5. I met him *at the station*. 我在車站遇見他。

其他常用的地方副詞有：here '這裏'、everywhere '到處'、outside '在外面'、inside '在裏面'、at school '在學校'、，in the kitchen '在廚房' 等。

地方副詞可以作 Where 起首的 Wh-問句的回應。例如：

> 6. A: *Where* did he go?
>   B: He went *upstairs*.(或 *Upstairs*)
> 7. A: *Where* did she stay?
>   B: She stayed *at home*.(或 *At home*.)

17.2.3.　時間副詞

(1)時間副詞表示動作之時間, 通常置於句末。常用的時間副詞如 yester-day '昨天'、now '現在'、today '今天'、afterwards '以後'、lately '近來'、soon '不久'、two weeks ago '兩星期以前'、for an hour '一個鐘頭' 等。例如:

1. He came *yesterday*. 他昨天來了。

2. She is studying *now.* 她現在正在唸書。

3. James wrote me a letter *a week ago.* James 一星期以前寫了一封信給我。

(2)有些時間動詞如 lately '近來'、recently '近來'、soon '不久'、already '已經'、immediately '馬上' 等可以置於動詞組的第一個字(即助動詞)後面。例如:

4. She has *recently* bought a dog. 她最近買了一隻狗。

5. We will *soon* move to a new apartment. 我們不久就會搬到一所新公寓去。

但如句子是否定時, 這些副詞通常仍置於句末。例如:

6. She hasn't bought a dog *recently.* 她最近沒有買一隻狗。

(3)時間副詞置於 *be* 後面, 但置於其他動詞(尤其是否定動詞)的前面。例如:

7. He is *still* here. 他還在這兒。

8. She *still* doesn't want to help us. 她還是不想幫助我們。

(4) *already* 與 *yet*

already 主要用於肯定句，*yet* 主要用於問句及否定句。例如：

9. I have **already** finished doing my homework. 我早已做完功課了。

10. Have you seen our new teacher **yet**? 你見過我們的新老師沒有？

11. He hasn't arrived **yet**. 他還沒有到達。

(5)時間副詞可以作 When 起首的 Wh—問句的回應。例如：

12. A: **When** did he come?

    B: He came **yesterday**. (或 **Yesterday**.)

17.2.4.　頻率副詞

(1)頻率副詞表示動作的次數/頻率，單字頻率副詞常置於 be 動詞後面，一般動詞前面；片語形式的頻率副詞則常置於句末。常用的頻率副詞如 never '從不'、seldom '很少'、sometimes '有時'、often '常常'、usually '通常'、always '總是'、twice a day '一天兩次'、three times a week '一週三次'、every day '每天' 等。例如：

1. He is **never** late. 他從不遲到。

2. They are **usually** on time. 他們通常準時。

3. John is **always** polite. John 總是有禮貌的。

4. We **seldom** go downtown. 我們很少到市中心鬧區去。

5. We go to school **every day**. 我們每天上學。

注意：sometimes 與 often 也可置於句末。例如：

He *sometimes* comes to see us. 他有時候來看我們。

He comes to see us *sometimes*.

⑵頻率副詞可作 How often 起首的 Wh-問句的回應。例如:

6. A: *How often* do we go to school?

B: We go to school *every day*.(或 *Every day*.)

17.2.5. 程度副詞

⑴程度副詞又稱爲「**強調詞**」(intensifier),通常修飾形容詞或另一副詞,置於其前面,表示其強弱的程度(如「**很**」、「**非常**」、「**極端**」等)。常用的程度副詞有 very、much、so、too、almost、enough、just、nearly、hardly、far、barely 等。例如:

1. She wrote the letter *very* carefully. 她很小心地寫這封信。

2. Joan is *too* selfish. Joan 太自私了。

注意: *enough* 置於其修飾的形容詞或副詞之後。例如: big *enough* '夠大'、fast *enough* '夠快'。

⑵ *much* 與 *far* 常與**比較級**或 *too*＋**原級**連用。例如:

3. Lesson Ten is *much/far* more difficult than Lesson One. 第十課比第一課困難很多。

4. This ring is *far/much* too expensive. 這戒指太貴了。

⑶ *almost*、*nearly*、*hardly*、*little*、*much* 等也可以修飾動詞。除 *much* 以外,通常置於動詞之前。例如:

5. She *almost* succeeded. 她幾乎成功了。

6. I *nearly* fell. 我差點跌倒。

7. We don't like her *much*. 我們不很喜歡她。

17.2.6.　句副詞

有些副詞並不修飾句子中任何語詞，而是修飾全句的句意，常表示說話者對句子所表達的意思所持的看法。這些副詞我們稱爲「**句副詞**」(sentence adverb)。句副詞常置於句首，也常用逗點與句子分開。例如：

1. *Luckily*, we arrived on time. 很幸運地，我們準時抵達了。

2. *Certainly*, I will help you. 我一定會幫助你。

3. *Obviously*, he is tired. 明顯地，他累了。

其他常用的句副詞有：honestly '老實地'、perhaps '也許'、frankly '坦白地'、naturally '自然地'、fortunately '幸運地' 等。

17.2.7.　同一句子中副詞的順序

同一句子中，如用上兩個或兩個以上的副詞時，一般的順序是：**地方副詞＞狀態副詞＞頻率副詞＞時間副詞**。例如：

1. John came *here this morning.* John 今天早上來過這兒。

2. He put the box *on the desk carefully a few minutes ago.* 他幾分鐘前把箱子小心地放在桌子上。

3. She talked to me *three times this morning.* 她今天早上跟我談了三次。

4. They stood *there quietly.* 他們靜靜地站在那兒。

注意：(a)上面的順序只是一般的常用順序，並非絕對不可改變的。

(b)上面順序中所列之「**頻率副詞**」不包括 always、usually、

often、sometimes、never、rarely 等字。這些字還是置於普通動詞之前或 be 動詞之後。

7.3.　副詞的形式與語意

⑴很多副詞都是在形容詞之後加-ly 詞尾而成。例如：

quick 快	quickly
slow 慢	slowly
happy 快樂	happily
possible 可能	possibly 等。

⑵有些形容詞與其相對的副詞在字形上完全不同。如 good(形)、well(副)。有些形容詞如 friendly '友善的'、lonely '寂寞的' 等則沒有相對的單字形式的副詞(亦即沒有*friendlyly 等字)。要表示副詞之意時，我們只能說 in a friendly manner '友善地'、in a lonely manner '寂寞地'。

⑶有些副詞同時具有-ly 與沒有-ly 形式。但其語意經常不相同。例如：

1. a. He works **hard**. 他努力地工作。

　b. He **hardly** works. 他幾乎不工作。

2. a. They arrived **late**. 他們遲到了(來晚了)

　b. I haven't seen him **lately**. 近來我沒看見過他。

類似的副詞有：

close	靠近	closely	細心地
near	不遠	nearly	幾乎
high	高	highly	極為、十分

17.4. 副詞的比較

17.4.1. 形式

(1)副詞比較級及最高級的形式與形容詞相似。單音節副詞加-er、-est 構成比較級及最高級。例如：

原級	比較級	最高級
hard 努力地	harder	hardest
early 早	earlier	earliest
high 高	higher	highest

(2)兩音節或更長的副詞加 more 及 most 構成比較級及最高級。例如：

| clearly 清楚地 | more clearly | most clearly |
| comfortably 舒服地 | more comfortably | most comfortably |

(3)另外，有些副詞比較形式的變化是不規則的。例如：

原級	比較級	最高級
well 好	better	best
badly 不好	worse	worst
much 多	more	most
little 少	less	least

far 遠 　　{ farther 　　{ farthest
　　　　　{ further 　　{ furthest

17.4.2. 副詞的比較句式

　　副詞的比較句式與形容詞的比較句式相似。詳細規則參看第十六章 16. 4.節。例如:

1. Vicky run *as fast as* Anna. Vicky 跑得像 Anna 一樣的快。(同等程度的比較)

2. She works *harder than* he. 她比他更努力工作。(較優的比較)

3. He works *less efficiently* than she. 他工作比她效率低。(較劣的比較)

4. Peter *works most* (*least*) *efficiently* of all. Peter 工作在所有人當中最有(沒有)效率。(三者以上的比較)

5. He is running *faster and faster*. 他跑得愈來愈快。(減增的比較)

6. *The earlier* he gets up, *the more efficiently* he works. 他早上愈早起工作就愈有效率。(對稱的比較)

17.5. 副詞的文法功能

　　副詞在句子中主要有以下幾種功能:

(1)修飾動詞。例如:
　1. He runs *fast*. 他跑得快。

2. She dances *well*. 她跳舞跳得好。

(2)修飾形容詞。例如:

1. She is *very* diligent. 她很勤勉。
2. This room is *rather* small. 這房間頗小。

(3)修飾另一個副詞。例如:

1. They will come *very* soon. 他們很快就會來。
2. She spoke *extremely* slowly. 她說得極慢。

以上三種是副詞主要的功能。以下是其他的一些次要功能:

(4)修飾介詞及介副詞。例如:

1. I left them *well* behind. 我把他們遠遠地留在後面。
2. The bullet went *right* through his arm. 子彈直穿他的手臂。

(5)修飾不定代名詞、數詞等。例如:

1. *Almost*/*Nearly* everyone came to my birthday party. 幾乎每個人都參加了我的生日會。
2. I have talked to *about*/*roughly* half the students. 我已經與大約半數的學生談過話了。
3. *Over* three hundred students were absent yesterday. 昨天有超過三百個學生缺席。

(6)有些時間副詞及地方副詞可以置於名詞後面,作名詞的修飾語。例如:

the day *before*　前一天
the meeting *yesterday*　昨天的會議

my trip *abroad*　我國外的旅行
his trip *home*　他回家的行程
your friends *there*　你在那邊的朋友
the examples *below*　下列的例子

17.6. 副詞移句首與倒裝

有些副詞移至句首時，句子中的主詞與動詞要倒裝，亦即變爲「**動詞＋主詞**」的詞序。最常見的情形有：

⑴副詞 away、down、in、out、off、over、around、up 等與表示動向的動詞連用時，可移至句首，其後的詞序變爲「**動向動詞＋主詞**」。例如：

　1.a. The students went *away*. 學生們走了。

　　b. *Away* went the students.

　2.a. The tree fell *down*. 樹倒下來。

　　b. *Down* fell the tree.

⑵有些含否定語意或限制性語意的副詞如 never、only、not until 等，因爲要加強語氣而移至句首時，句子的主詞與助動詞要倒裝，如沒有助動詞時，要加上適當的 do 動詞，再與主詞倒裝。例如：

　1.a. She *never* visits her uncle. 她從來都不探望她叔叔。

　　b. *Never does she* visit her uncle.

　2.a. He can communicate with us *only* by writing. 他只能以書寫的方式來跟我們通訊。

　　b. *Only by writing can he* communicate with us.

17.7. 有關副詞的其他注意事項

(1) *very* 與 *much*

much(如前不加 very)通常用於否定句及問句，但 very 則沒有這種限制。例如：

　　1. He doesn't swim *much* these days. 這些日子裏他不常游泳。

　　2. Does he swim *much* lately? 最近他常游泳嗎？

另外，much 可以修飾比較級，但 very 不可以。例如：

　　3. She felt *much* better. 她覺得好多了。(不可以說*very better)

(2) *every day* 與 *everyday*

everyday 是形容詞；副詞為 every day，要分開寫。例如：

　　1. These are my *everyday* shoes. 這些是我平日穿的鞋子。

　　2. I go to school *every day*. 我每天上學去。

(3) *sometime, sometimes, some time*

sometime 是副詞，表示‘在某一時間’；*sometimes* 也是副詞表示‘有時候’；*some time* 是名詞組，表示‘一段時間’。例如：

　　1. I saw her *sometime* last month. 我上個月(某天)見過她。

　　2. We must get together *sometime* next week. 下週我們得找個時間聚一聚。

　　3. He *sometimes* goes to church. 他有時候(偶而，並非經常)去教堂。

　　4. Can you spare me *some time*? 你能勻出一些時間給我嗎？

⑷ *maybe* 與 *may be*

maybe 是副詞，意思是'或許/也許'（＝perhaps）；*may be* 是**助動詞＋*be***，意思是'可能/可能是'（＝be possible）。例如：

1. *Maybe* she will come tomorrow. 也許她明天會來。

2. He *may be* interested in our plan. 他可能對我們的計畫感興趣。

《習題 21》

(A)寫出以下各項形容詞相對的副詞。

例：happy：*happily*

1. good： _____   2. beautiful： _____

3. fast： _____   4. physical： _____

5. brave： _____   6. glad： _____

7. serious： _____   8. simple： _____

9. usual ： _____   10. certain： _____

11. quiet： _____   12. careful： _____

(B)將括號中的副詞置於最常用的位置。

例：He sang. (loudly)

He sang *loudly*.

1. Mary got up. (early)

2. We came home. (late)

3. He fought the battle. (bravely)

4. She wrote the story. (descriptively '描述性地')

5. He graduated from high school. (last year)

(C)將下列頻率副詞置於正確位置。

例： a.He is late. (never)

He is *never* late.

b.He comes home late. (never)

He *never* comes home late.

1. She goes shopping at night. (sometimes)

2. We go to church on Sunday. (always)

3. She goes to the movies alone. (seldom)

4. He is nervous. (sometimes)

5. She is busy. (often)

6. Anne is kind to us. (always)

7. He talks loudly. (seldom)

8. Albert is late for class. (usually)

(D)將括號中的副詞置於動詞組的第一個助動詞後面。

例： He will work hard. (always)

He will *always* work hard.

1. He is washing the dishes. (carefully)

2. I have told him not to come here. (already)

3. This room is decorated (裝飾). (nicely)

4. Have you seen a tiger? (ever)

5. He will come on time. (certainly)

(E)將下列每句後括號中的副詞以適當的順序置於句子中。

例： He came. (once a week, here)

　　He came *here* *once a week*.

1. He has lived. (for one year, in Taipei)

2. They talked (at the front door, loudly, this morning)

3. I take a walk. (sometimes, in the evening, along the road)

4. I drink tea. (in the afternoon, seldom)

5. I sent a letter. (yesterday, to London, by air mail)

6. He goes. (sometimes, alone, in the afternoon, to the movies)

7. Lilly called Helen. (yesterday, a few times)

8. It snows. (here, in winter, never)

9. We have our dinner. (usually, at 7:00, here)

10. He went. (last year, to New York)

(F)將下列數句副詞移至句首，並調整主詞與動詞的詞序。

　　例： a. The boy went away.

　　　　 Away went the boy.

　　　 b. I have never seen him like that.

　　　　 Never have I seen him like that.

1. Some apples fell down.

2. Tom comes here.

3. Mary went into the room.

4. The children sat around the fire.

5. I have never seen such a naughty boy.

6. You can succeed only in this way.

(G)選出正確的項目。

1. John has (a. already, b. yet) done his homework.

2. He has not (a. already, b. yet) come.

3. They were talking about (a. the meeting yesterday, b. the yesterday meeting).

4. She felt (a. very, b. much) better after she took some medicine.

5. The book is not (a. very, b. much) interesting.

6. She goes to the movies (a. every day, b. everyday).

7. Mr. Johnson is (a. far, b. very) too busy.

8. (a. May be, b. Maybe) I'll buy you a diamond ring.

第十八章
介詞

18.1. 介詞簡說

　　英語中的**介詞**(preposition)是一種沒有詞尾或其他字形變化的字，置於名詞或名詞相等語之前，表示「**時間**」、「**處所**」、「**方向**」、「**狀態**」、「**原因**」、「**方法**」、「**結果**」、「**程度**」等語意功能。

　　介詞又稱爲「**介系詞**」或「**前置詞**」，尾隨其後的名詞或名詞相等語稱爲介詞的**受詞**(object of preposition)，爲受格。因此，如介詞後面是代名詞時，用受格形式(例如：for him, to them 等)。介詞與尾隨的名詞構成「**介詞片語**」。以下是一些含介詞的例句：

　　1. He will come ***on*** Sunday. 他星期天會來。

　　2. They arrived ***in*** Hong Kong. 他們到達香港。

　　3. The book ***on*** the desk is mine. 桌上的書是我的。

　　「**介詞片語**」在文法上常具有副詞或形容詞的功能。以上例句1的 ***on*** Sunday 具有時間副詞的功能，修飾動詞 will come。例句2的 ***in*** Hong Kong 具有地方副詞的功能，修飾 arrived。例句3的 ***on*** the desk 具有形容詞的功能，修飾 the book。

　　介詞的分類很難做到完善，但是以其表達的語意功能來劃分，在教與學的過程上具有實用的價值，也能幫助學生記憶。以下我們就以這種語意上的分類法來介紹介詞的用法。

18.2. 介詞的種類

18.2.1. 表示時間的介詞

⑴ **on**、**at**、**in** 都可表示某一時間，但用法不同。
　⒜ **on** 與日或日期(day/date)連用；
　⒝ **at** 通常與某一時間、年紀(a time/age)連用；
　⒞ **in** 通常與早上、下午、晚上、星期、月、季、年等(morning/afternoon/evening/week/month/season/year 等)連用。

例如：

1. He arrived **in** the morning. 他早上到達。
2. Anna was born **on** September 1, 1948. Anna 出生於公元 1948 年 9 月 1 日。
3. I graduated from junior high school **in** 1978. 我 1978 年國中畢業。
4. She will see us **at** 8:30 tomorrow morning. 她明天八點半將會接見我們。
5. Tom got married **at** forty-five. Tom 在 45 歲的時候結婚。

　　其他常用的例子有：**at** night '晚上'、**at** six o'clock '六點鐘'、**at** midnight '半夜'、**at** noon '中午'、**at** this moment '這一刻'、**at** that time '那時候'、*at* Christmas '在聖誕節的時候' 等。

　　on Sunday '在星期天'、*on* July 4 '在七月四日那天'、*on* Christmas day '在聖誕節當天'、*on* Monday morning '在星期一早上'、*on* the morning of June 10 '在六月十日的早上'、*on* halidays '在假日'、*on* new year's Eve '在除夕' 等。

　　in October '在十月'、*in* 1957 '在 1957 年'、*in* the evening '在晚上'、*in* (the) spring '在春天'、*in* my childhood '在我的童年' 等。

　　(2) *since*、*by*、*from* ... *to* (*until*/*till*)...、*for*、*during*、*in*/*within* 等表示一段時間/時期。例如：

　　　1. He has been living here *since* 1961. 他自從 1961 年以來一直都住在這兒。

　　　2. We usually work *from* 9:00 a.m. *to* (*untill*/*till*) 5:00 p.m. 我們通常從早上九點工作到下午五點。

　　　3. I have not seen him *for* three years. 我三年沒見過他了。

　　　4. She will finish writing the report *by* the end of this month. 本月底以前她將會把報告寫好。

　　　5. I'll be back *in* an hour. 我一個鐘頭內會回來。

　　　6. She swam a lot *during* the summer vacation. 暑期裏她常游泳。

　　注意：(a) *during* 與 *in* 都可表示一段時間，通常也可以通用，但 *during* 比較強調完整的一段時間。

　　　　　(b) *in, within* 與 *by* 與時間語調連用時，其語意上的分別是： *in* 與 *within* 表示「在…時間內」，*by* 表示「在…以前/不遲於 …」。例如：Larry learned to speak English *in*/*within* two years. '他兩年之內學會說英文'。I'll be back *by*

Sunday. '我星期天以前會回來'。但 *in*＋**時間**用語也可以表示**在…之後／在…之末」**。例如：The house will be completed *in* a year. '這房子一年就會建好'。I'll see you *in* an hour. '我一小時後見你'。

(c) *in* time **表示** '**及時**'、*on* time **表示** '**準時**'。

(d) *since*＋**時間**用語常與完成時式連用。例如：I *haven't seen* him *since* last Monday.

(3)表示先後的介詞有 *after*、*before* 等。例如：

1. I'll send you a letter *before* Monday. 我會在星期一以前寄一封信給你。

2. She likes to watch TV *after* dinner. 晚飯以後她喜歡看電視。

18.2.2. 表示處所的介詞

(1) *in*、*at*、*on*：

in 常與比較大的地方語詞(如大城市、國家等)連用。

at 常與表示較小的地方語詞(如車站、機場、辦公室等)連用。

表示街道時，*on* 與街道名稱連用，*at* 與門牌號碼連用。例如：

1. She lives *in* Taipei. 她住在臺北。

2. He is now *in* France. 他現在在法國。

3. I saw him *at* the airport yesterday. 我昨天在機場看見他。

4. They live *on* Chi Nan Road. 他們住在濟南路。

5. He lived *at* 1177 West 28th Street. 她住在西二十八街1177號。

6. I'll see you *at* my office. 我將會在我的辦公室見你。

另外，*on* 表在「在上」(在某物表面之上，與這物件接觸)，*in* 表示「在內」，*at* 表示「在某地點」或其鄰近之處。例如：

> *in* the roon 在房間裏
>
> *on* the table 在桌上
>
> *at* the store 在那家商店

(2) *above* 與 *over* 表示「在…上方」，常可通用。例如：

1. The kite was right *over*/*above* our heads. 風箏正好在我們頭頂上方。

2. The helicopter hovered *above*/*over* the tree. 這直升機在樹上方盤旋。

但要表示「覆蓋」、「在另一邊」、「橫/跨過」時，只能用 *over*。例如：

3. He lives *over* the mountains. 他住在山的那一邊。

4. She put a blanket *over* the old woman. 她把一條毯子蓋在那個老婦人身上。

5. There is a small bridge *over* the stream. 那條小溪上有座小橋。

(3) *below* 與 *under* 都可表示「在…之下」、「比…低」，常可通用。但通常 *under* 表示有所接觸，而 *below* 常表示兩者之間有空間，不直接接觸。例如：

1. I put the ring *under* the pillow. 我把戒指放在枕頭下面。

2. They live on the *floor* below us. 他們住在我們下面的一層樓。(試比較：They live on the floor *above* us. 他們住在我們上面的一層樓。)

其他表示地方的介詞有: **beside** '在旁邊'、**behind** '在後面'、**opposite** '在對面'、**against** '對着/靠着' 等。例如:

1. She is standing **behind** the door. 她站在門後。
2. John is leaning **against** the wall. John 正在靠着牆上。

18.2.3. 表示方向/動向的介詞

常用的表示方向/動向的介詞有: **to**、**from**、**at**、**into**、**out of**、**toward**(**s**)、**away from**、**up**、**down**、**around**、**through**、**past**、**by**、**as far as**、**up to** 等。例如:

1. He walked **into** the classroom. 他走進教室。
2. He went **from** Taichung **to** Taipei. 他從臺中到臺北去。
3. Paula rushed **out of** the room. Paula 從房間衝出來。
4. The senator walked **toward**(**s**) the crowd. 參議員朝着群衆走過去。
5. They went **up**(**down**) the stairs. 他們走樓梯上(下)去。

18.2.4. 表示狀態的介詞

表示狀態的介詞常用的有: **with**、**like**、**in**、**on**、**by** 等。例如:

1. He walks **like** a girl. 他走起路來像個女孩子。
2. She washed the silk dress **with** care. 她小心地洗那件絲質洋裝。
3. Eric goes to school **on** foot. Eric 走路上學。
4. He came here **by** taxi. 他坐計程車來這兒。
5. She told me the news **in** whisper. 她以耳語的方式把那件消

息告訴我。

18.2.5. 其他的語意

⑴**原因或理由或目的**：*for*、*because of*、*out of* 等。

1. I bought the car *for* him. 我買這部車子給他。（＝爲他而買的）
2. She left early *because of* her headache. 她因爲頭疼而提早走了。
3. They helped her *out of* sympathy. 他們是爲了同情而幫助她。
4. We did it *for* fun. 我們是爲了好玩而做這事的。

⑵**結果**：*into*、*out of* 等。

1. My wife talked me *into* buying a new car. 我太太說服我買了一部新汽車。
2. She also talked me *out of* selling the house. 她也說服我不賣那幢房子。

⑶**伴隨/陪伴**：*with*

1. I am going *with* you. 我跟你一起去。

⑷**工具**：*with*

1. She cut the apple *with* a knife. 她用刀子切蘋果。
2. He bought the car *with* his own money. 他用自己的錢來買這部車子。

⑸功能/能力: *as*

1. She did her job well *as* a teacher. 作爲一位老師，她很稱職。
2. A prepositional phrase can be used *as* an adverb. 介詞片詞可以當作副詞使用。

⑹量度: *at*、*by*

1. The plane is flying *at* 600 miles an hour. 這飛機正以時速600哩飛行。
2. The meat is sold *by* the pound. 這肉以磅爲單位出售。

⑺主事者: *by*

1. This book was written *by* my father. 這本書是我父親寫的。

18.3.　介詞與其他詞類連用

18.3.1.　介詞與動詞

介詞與動詞常組合成「**片語動詞**」。常用的動詞與介詞與受詞的組合有:

⑴**動詞＋介詞**。例如:

    add to 增加   *agree on* 同意
    agree with someone *on* something 在某事上與某人同意
    argue with 辯論、辯駁   *ask for* 請求

arrive at 到達　　　　　*belong to* 屬於

believe in 相信　　　　*complain about* 抱怨

depend on 依靠　　　　*hear from* 得知、知道消息

laugh at 取笑、嘲笑　　*think of/about* 想到

wait for 等待　　　　　*look at* 看

talk about 談及

1. They *arrived at* the airport. 他們到達機場。

2. Mary *laughed at* Tom. Mary 嘲笑 Tom。

3. They *are looking at* the pictures. 他們正在看那些畫。

4. They never *complain about* anything. 他們對任何事情從來都不抱怨。

⑵動詞＋受詞＋介詞。例如：

blame ... for ... 　因…而責備…

compare ... with ... 　以…與…比較

explain ... to ... 　向…解釋…

fill ... with ... 　把…注滿…

help ... with ... 　幫…做…

introduce ... to ... 　把…介紹給…

translate ... into ... 　把…翻譯成…　等。

1. Can you *explain* this sentence *to* me?　你可以把這個句子解釋給我聽嗎？

2. Can you *translate* this sentence *into* Chinese?　你可以把這個句子翻譯成中文嗎？

3. He should *help* his mother *with* housework. 他應該幫忙他媽媽做家事。

18.3.2.　介詞與形容詞

與形容詞(包括分詞)連用的介詞常用的有:

afraid of 害怕　　　　　　*according to* 根據

angry with 生氣　　　　　*ashamed of* 羞愧

capable of 有能力　　　　*different from* 不同

full of 充滿　　　　　　　*good at* 精於

interested in 感興趣　　　*late for* 遲到

pleased with 高興　　　　*proud of* 引以為榮

tired of 倦於　　　　　　*used to* 慣於

welcome to 歡迎

1. She is *afraid of* her uncle. 她怕她叔叔。

2. He is always *late for* work. 他上班老是遲到。

3. She is *interested in* studying English. 她對研讀英文感興趣。

4. Your book is *different from* mine. 你的書與我的不同。

18.3.3.　介詞與名詞

名詞與介詞的組合與動詞或形容詞與介詞的組合不同。名詞不只可以置於介詞前面(如 interest in),也可置於介詞的後面(如 in fact)。

⑴名詞＋介詞。例如:

application for 申請　　　*answer to* 答案

interest in 興趣　　　　　*key to* 解答

arrival at 到達　　　　　　*confidence in* 信心　等。

1. She has great *interest in* popular music. 她對流行音樂有很大的興趣。

2. I know the *answer to* this question. 我知道這個問題的答案。

(2)介詞＋名詞。例如：

in case 萬一、如果　　　*in fact* 事實上

at ease 從容、舒坦　　　*on vacation* 渡假　等。

1. *In fact,* they are very rich. 事實上，他們很有錢。

2. The Huangs are *on vacation* now. 黃家全家現在正在渡假。

《習題 22》

(A)選出正確項目。

1. He should keep the keys (in, on) the drawer(抽屜).

2. Janet wanted to stay (with, on) her aunt.

3. The store is (near, on) the supermarket.

4. We will see our teacher off(送行)(on, at) the airport tomorrow.

5. John lives (at, on) Chung Shan North Road.

6. Jane lives (in, at) 152, Chi Nan Road.

7. The fast food restaurant is (above, across) the street.

8. Tommy is now leaning (around, against) the wall.

9. Bob was sitting (at, in) the chair.

10. He lived (in, on) Europe during the war.

11. Did she stay (at, on) your place last night?

12. Did you read about the story (in, on) that book?

(B)選出正確的項目。

1. He is taking a nap(午睡)(in, on, at) the middle of the day.

2. The movie starts (on, in, at) 7:30 p.m..

3. She often eats lunch (on, in, at) noon.

4. Mr. Smith is going to teach a new course(in, on, until) September.

5. We will wait for him (since, until) twelve o'clock.

6. I haven't seen her (until, in, since) last October.

7. He will have finished writing his story (in, at, by) the end of this week.

8. A: When will he come?

　B: He will come (in, at, on) the evening.

9. I'll be back (in, around, at) about half an hour.

10. Don't worry. We'll be there (about, at, on) time.

11. Come in. You're just (at, in) time for tea.

12. Anna will go to church (in, on) Sunday morning.

(C)填入適當的介詞。

1. The bell rang _____ midnight.

2. _____ the storm, the lights in the house went out(熄滅) _____ several hours.

3. I am going to wait for them _____ the lobby(飯店的大廳)of the hotel.

4. She'll meet me _____ the station.

5. Mary kept laughing _____ Terry.

6. Don't look _____ me like that. You're making me nervous.

7. He was absent _____ school yesterday.

8. I will not talk _____ anything that I do not understand.

9. He cut the apple _____ a knife.

10. I went to school _____ foot yesterday.

11. But Mary went to school _____ bus.

12. Don't blame me _____ not helping Nancy.

13. He just did it _____ fun.

14. The meat is sold _____ the pound.

15. Noel is working here _____ a secretary.

16. I can see you _____ my office now.

17. He is driving _____ 60 miles an hour.

18. I will tell you this _____ whisper.

19. He came to work for us _____ 1968.

20. He bought a present _____ her.

(D)填入適當的介詞。

1. He tried very hard to argue _____ me.

2. Would you please listen _____ me?

3. Very young children depend _____ their parents for almost everything.

4. I am not afraid _____ Tom.

5. I am ashamed _____ you.

6. This bottle is full _____ water.

7. He is good _____ physics(物理).

8. This is a very good answer _____ your question.

9. She has no interest _____ English at all.

10. What is she really interested _____ ?

(E)將以下各句之錯誤介詞找出，並改正過來。

例：He comes _in_ Sunday. (×)

　　He comes _on_ Sunday.

1. David lives on 15 Hsin Yi Road, Section I.

2. John received a letter by his best friend.

3. Please read aloud from line 5 into line 10 in page 15.

4. We have to go to school in foot every day.

5. You can always depend in us.

6. She has been waiting for Louis at two o'clock in the afternoon.

7. The book is in the shelf.

8. Theory(理論)is different than practice(實行).

第十九章
不定詞

19.1. 簡介不定詞、分詞、及動名詞

英語的普通動詞除了獨立使用的完整動詞形式以外，還有「不定詞」(infinitive)、「分詞」(participle)、以及「動名詞」(gerund)三種形式。例如：

不定詞	分詞	動名詞
work	to work	working	working
		worked	

這三種形式都是由動詞衍生的，也保留了動詞的一些特性，例如可以有受詞(to speak *English* '說英語'，也可以被副詞修飾(to speak English *fluently* '流利地說英語')。然而，在文法功能上，這幾種形式都不當作動詞使用。其真正的文法功能是當作名詞、形容詞、或副詞使用。例如：

1. *To speak English* is not difficult. 說英語並不難。(不定詞作 is 的主詞)
2. *Grass skiing* is my favorite. 滑草是我喜愛的運動(動名詞作 is 的主詞)
3. I have a composition *to write*. 我有一篇作文要寫。(不定詞

作形容詞, 修飾 composition)

4. We don't have **running** water here. 我們這兒沒有自來水。
(現在分詞作形容詞, 修飾 water)

5. He went to the supermarket **to buy some food**. 他到超級
市場去買一些食物。(不定詞作副詞, 修飾 went, 表示「去」的目的)

本章介紹不定詞, 以下第二十、二十一兩章分別介紹分詞與動名詞。

19.2. 不定詞的形式與結構

(1)不定詞的形式有以下幾種:

	主動		被動
	簡單	進行	
一般形式	*to give*	*to be giving*	*to be given*
完成形式	*to have given*	*to have been giving*	*to have been given*

一般形式表示與句子主動詞同時發生或是比主動詞較後才會發生的動
作。完成形式則表示早於主動詞的動作。

從上表也可知, 無論任何形式, 不定詞都含 **to**, 因此 **to** 可以說是不定
詞的標誌。

另外, 不定詞的否定形式是「**not＋不定詞**」, 例如: **not to give, not
to have given** 等。

(2)不定詞的結構

不定詞有以下五種結構：

> a. *to*＋V
>
> b. *to*＋V＋NP(obj)
>
> c. *to*＋V＋NP(obj)＋Adv
>
> d. (*for*＋NP) *to*＋V＋NP(obj)＋Adv
>
> e. NP(obj)＋*to*＋V

例如：

1. He likes *to speak.* 他喜歡說話。(a)

2. He likes *to speak English.* 他喜歡說英語。(b)

3. He wants *to speak English fluently.* 他想流利地說英語。(c)

4. It is not easy *for him to speak English fluently*. 他說英語, 不容易說得流利。(d)(＝For him to speak English fluently is not easy. ‘要他流利地說英語不是容易的事’)

5. I want *him to speak English*. 我想要他說英語。(e)

19.3. 不定詞的用法

19.3.1. 不定詞作名詞使用

⑴不定詞可作句子的主詞。句子的動詞通常是 *be*、*seem*、*appear* 等。例如：

1. *For John to fail in the test* was unfortunate. John 考試不及格, 真是不幸。

2. *For her to work hard* seems impossible. 要她用功似乎不可能。

3. *To work hard* is advisable. 用功是明智的。

4. *To build a new house* often costs a lot of money. 建一幢新房子通常花費很多錢。

5. *To see his children again* makes him happy. 再見到他的孩子們使他很高興。

以上1～5的說法比較正式,常用的說法是用引導詞 *it* 取代不定詞,然後將不定詞移至句末。(有關引導詞 it 的用法,參看第二十五章。)例如:

6. *It* was unfortunate *for John to fail in the test.*(=1)

7. *It* seems impossible *for her to work hard.*(=2)

8. *It* is advisable *to work hard.*(=3)

9. *It* often costs a lot of money *to build a new house.*(=4)

10. *It* makes him happy *to see his children again.*(=5)

⑵不定詞可作句子的受詞。其句型有兩種。

⒜「**主詞＋動詞＋不定詞**」

這句式中,句子的主詞同時也是不定詞的「**主詞**」,亦即做不定詞的動作的人。下列動詞常用於這種句式:

agree	同意	afford	負擔
arrange	安排	ask	要求
forget	忘記	hate	憎恨、很不喜歡
hope	希望	begin	開始
decide	決定	refuse	拒絕
start	開始	love	喜愛
mean	意欲、打算	plan	計劃

prefer	比較喜歡	promise	答應
try	嘗試	want	想要
wish	希望 等。		

例如:

1. I want *to buy a new car*. 我想買一部新汽車。

2. They tried *to keep quiet*. 他們試著不作聲。

3. Betty promised *to send her daughter a letter*. Betty 答應要給她的女兒寫一封信。

⒝「主詞＋動詞＋NP＋不定詞」

在這句式中，NP 是句子主動詞的受詞，同時也是不定詞的「主詞」。因此句子的主詞與做不定詞的動作的人並不相同。下列動詞常用於這種句式:

*ask	要求	allow	允許
*prepare	準備	cause	導致
require	需要	request	請求
*expect	期望	teach	教
*want	想要	tell	告訴、吩咐
*wish	希望	get	使、導致
force	強迫	order	命令
permit	允許	invite	邀請 等。

(打*號的動詞也可用於⒜之句式)

例如:

1. He wanted her *to be on time*. 他想要她準時。

2. I invited her *to come to my party*. 我邀請她參加我的聚會。

3. We forced him *to sell the stamps*. 我們強迫他把郵票賣掉。

這些句子與⒜的句子不同，這句式可以改成被動句。例如:

4. He was forced (by us) to sell the stamps. 他被(我們所)迫把郵票賣掉。

(3)不定詞可作補語

(A)在 *be*、*seem*、*appear* 後面，做主詞補語。例如：

1. I am *not to blame*. 不能怪我。
2. He appears *to be happy*. 他看起來很快樂。
3. She seems *to be in a hurry*. 她似乎很匆忙。

(B)在 *believe*、*find*、*prove*、*show*、*think*、*suppose* 等動詞後面做受詞補語，不定詞主要是 to be。例如：

1. We believe her *to be a good student*. 我們相信她是個好學生。
2. Her friends think her *to be a good mother.* 她的朋友們認為她是個好母親。
3. The police proved him *to be innocent.* 警方證實他是清白的。

19.3.2. 不定詞作形容詞使用

不定詞可置於名詞後面，當形容詞使用，修飾該名詞。例如：

1. He has a plan *to study French.* 他有一個唸法文的計畫。
2. There is no one *to help us.* 沒有人要幫助我們。
3. We have enough food *to eat.* 我們有足夠的食物可吃。
4. Do you have anything *to tell me*? 你有任何事情要告訴我嗎？

5. He has a lot of time *to do his homework.* 他有很多時間做功課。

19.3.3. 不定詞作副詞使用

⑴修飾動詞

不定詞修飾動詞時，最常用的功能是表示「目的」，表示「目的」的不定詞通常置於動詞後面，其形式有「to＋V」、「*in order to*＋V」、「*so as to*＋V」。例如：

1. We come here *to study.* 我們來這兒唸書。
2. I moved closer to the blackboard *in order to see the words on it more clearly.* 我向黑板靠近些，爲了要看得更清楚在上面的字。
3. They took a taxi *so as to save time.* 他們坐計程車是爲了想省時間。

⑵不定詞修飾述語形容詞

下列形容詞後面可接不定詞，作其修飾語。

afraid	害怕	careful	小心
certain	確定	eager	渴望
glad	高興	easy	容易
difficult	困難	hard	困難
happy	高興	proud	自豪
ready	準備好	sorry	不安
sure	確定 等。		

例如：

1. He is afraid *to see his boss.* 他怕見他的老闆。

2. This exercise is easy *to do.* 這個練習很容易做。

3. I am happy *to be here.* 我很高興來到這兒。

有時候，有些形容詞如 easy、difficult 等，後面也可以加 *for*＋NP＋不定詞。例如：This exercise is easy *for us to do.* '這練習對我們而言很容易做'。

⑶不定詞可修飾與 *too*、*enough*、以及 *so ... as to* 連用的形容詞或副詞。這種不定詞常表示某種結果。例如：

1. He is *too busy to help me.* 他太忙而不能幫助我。（＝He is so busy that he cannot help me.）

2. The soup is *too hot to drink.* 這湯太熱了，不能喝。（＝The soup is so hot that we or he 等 can't drink it.）

3. She is *old enough to take care of herself.* 她年紀夠大了，可以照顧自己。（＝She is so old that she can take care of herself）

4. We walked *fast enough to get to school* on time. 我們走得夠快，而能準時到達學校。（＝We walked so fast that we could get to school on time.）

5. He was *so foolish as to lie to his boss.* 他笨到對他老闆撒謊。（＝He was so foolish that lied to his boss.）

⑷不定詞可修飾全句

修飾全句的不定詞通常置於句首，但也可置於句末。

1. *To be honest,* I don't like English. 老實的說，我不喜歡英文。

2. *To be frank*, you are not a good driver. 坦白的說，你不是一個好駕駛。

3. I have never liked you, *to tell you the truth.* 老實的跟你說，我從來都沒有喜歡你。

19.4. 不定詞的否定式、被動式、進行式、及完成式

⑴不定詞的否定式爲「*not*＋不定詞」。例如：

1. I'll try *not to be late.* 我會努力不遲到。

2. She decided *not to help Anna.* 她決定不幫助 Anna。

⑵不定詞的被動式爲「*to be*＋*V-en*(過去分詞)」或「*to have been*＋*V-en*(過去分詞)」。例如：

1. She didn't want *to be disturbed.* 她不想被打擾。

2. There is a lot of work *to be done.* 有很多事情要做。

3. She seems *to have been forgiven by her mother.* 她似乎已經被她母親原諒了。

注意：　(*a*) 如句子的主詞也是不定詞的「主詞」時，不能用被動式不定詞。例如: I have a lot of work *to do.* '我有很多事情要做。'(I 是 have 的主詞也是做 to do 動作的主事者)。這一句就不能說成*I have a lot of work *to be done.*

　　　　(*b*) 例句2之主詞並非某一特別的主事者，因此，主動或被動式都可以用，There is a lot of work *to do/to be done.* 皆可。

(c)如句子的主詞是不定詞的受詞時，用被動式不定詞。例如:

These clothes are *to be washed.* '這些衣服是要洗的'
(這句不能說成*These clothes are to wash)。同理，例句
3 也不可以用主動式不定詞。

(3)進行式不定詞表示動作之持續性，形式爲「*to be＋V-ing*(現在分詞)」。例如:

It is nice *to be sitting* next to you. 坐在你旁邊眞好。

(4)完成式不定詞的形式爲「*to have＋V-en*(過去分詞)」表示早於句子主動詞之動作。而簡單式不定詞則表示與句子主動詞同時或稍後的動作。例如:

1. He seems *to be a good student.* 看來他是一個好學生。
2. He seems *to have been a good student.* 看來他當時(過去)是一個好學生。

一般說來，完成式的不定詞常與 *seem* '似乎、看來' 、*appear* '看起來' 、*mean* '本來想要' 等動詞連用。

19.5.　To 代替前面已經說過的不定詞

爲避免不必要的重覆，我們可以用 to 來代替前面已經說過的不定詞。這種用法常用於動詞 *hate* '不喜歡' 、*hope* '希望' 、*intend* '打算' 、*would like* '想' 、*would love* '想、很喜歡' 、*mean* '本來想' 、*plan* '計劃' 、*try* '試著' 、*want* '想要' 等後面。另外，*have to、need to、ought to、used to、be able to、be going to* 等也常用來避免重覆。例如:

1. He didn't come because he **didn't want to.** (=... didn't want to come.) 他沒有來, 因爲他不想來。

2. He didn't come because he **didn't have to.** (=... didn't have to come.) 他沒有來, 因爲他不必來。

3. A: Do you play the piano? 你彈鋼琴嗎?

   B: No, but I **used to.** (=... I used to play the piano.) 不, (我現在不彈了), 但我以前常彈。

19.6. how/what/when/where/ which/who+不定詞

這類不定詞片語通常置於動詞後面, 作受詞使用。例如:

1. He doesn't know **how to use a computer.** 他不知道如何使用電腦。

2. We could not decide **what to do next.** 我們不能決定下一步該做什麼。

3. Please tell me **when to turn off the lights.** 請告訴我什麼時候關燈。

4. Can you tell me **where to buy a shirt**? 你可以告訴我該到哪裏去買襯衫嗎?

5. She showed me **which way to go.** 她指示我該走哪一條路。

6. I don't know **who to invite.** 我不知道要邀請誰。

其他與「**wh+不定詞**」連用的動詞有 **ask**、**forget**、**remember**、**learn**、**wonder** 等。

19.7. 不定詞在結構及用法上應注意的事項

⑴表示「**目的**」的不定詞片語常可移句首,但不定詞與主句之間要用**逗點**(comma)。例如:

1. We changed our seats (*in order*) *to get a better view of the stage.* 我們換了座位, 爲的是要更清楚地看見舞臺。

2. (*In order*) *To get a better view of the stage*, we chang-ed our seat. 爲了要更清楚地看見舞臺, 我們換了座位。

⑵不定詞片語置於句首時, 如不定詞本身沒有「*for+NP*」時, 做不定詞動作的人也就是句子的主詞; 這時候, 我們要特別注意不定詞與句子主詞是否相容。如兩者不相容時, 就產生所謂「**誤連**」(misrelated; dangling)現象。這是我們要避免的。例如:

3. 正確: *To get a better view* of the stage, *we* changed our seat.(句意如例2)

4. 誤連: *＊To get a better view* of the stage, *our seats* were changed.＊爲了要更清楚地看見舞臺, 我們的座位被換了。

例句3的主詞是 we, 可以做 get a better view 的動作; 但例句4的主詞是 our seat, 座位是無生命之物, 不可能做 get a better view 的動作, 因此爲「**誤連**」的修飾語。以下例句5也是「**誤連**」的不定詞:

5. 誤連: *＊To explain the meaning* of the word more clearly, pictures were used. 爲了把這個字的意思解釋得更清楚, 圖片被使用上了。

例句5不妥當在於句子主詞 pictures 與不定詞 to explain 不相容,

'圖片' 不可能做 '解釋' 的動作。改成例句6之後就沒有問題了。

6. 正確: **To explain the meaning** of the word more clearly, **our teacher** used pictures. 爲了把這個字的意思解釋得更清楚，我們的老師使用了圖片。

(3)動詞 **let**、**make**、**have** 及感官動詞 **see**、**hear**、**watch** 等後面的不定詞不帶 to。例如:

1. **Let** me **go.** 讓我走。

2. She **made** me **laugh.** 她使我笑。

3. I **had** John **clean** the room. 我要 John 清理房間。

4. I **heard** the bell **ring.** 我聽到鈴響。

另外，動詞 help 後面可跟帶 to 或不帶 to 的不定詞。

5. I helped her **to solve**/**solve** the problem. 我幫她解決了這個問題

《習題23》

(A)在以下各句中，把不定詞找出來，如是簡單式以外的其他形式，請註明。

例: a. I want _to come_.

b. They appear _to be smiling_. (進行式)

c. They seemed _to have left it there_. (完成式)

d. She decided _not to go_. (否定式)

e. I gave her a letter _to be typed_. (被動式)

1. I expect to see my students soon.

2. She seems to have lost the money.

3. To understand is to forgive.

4. To see is to believe.

5. The flowers are to be put in the vase(花瓶).

6. I want to do this at once.

7. We believe there to have been an accident some time ago.

8. He seems to have understood all my questions.

9. He was foolish enough to have believed her.

10. We have just decided not to go to the movies.

11. She seems to be enjoying herself.

(B)在以下各句中，填入適當的不定詞。

    例：I want _____ .

    I want *to go to the movies*.

1. Don't forget _____ a letter to me.

2. David doesn't want _____ any money.

3. We decided not _____ .

4. I don't know what _____ .

5. We plan _____ baseball tomorrow.

6. I like _____ .

7. We want _____ her some flowers.

(C)利用不定詞來回答下列問題。

    例：What did he want to do?

    He wanted to study English.

1. Did you forget to bring your book?

2. What did he tell you to do?

3. Do you wish to have a daughter?

4. Who would like to work overtime(加班)?

5. Have you learn how to drive a car?

6. What did he expect(期望) you to do?

(D)將括號中的單字寫成一個不定詞片語，使成爲句子的主詞。

　例： a. (I/get up/early) is easy.

　　　　For me to get up early is easy.

　　　 b. (change/a/tire) is not easy.

　　　　To change a tire is not easy.

1. (She/win/the race) is not easy.

2. (answer/this question) is very difficult.

3. (hire/an/experienced(有經驗的)/person) is advisable(明智的).

4. (live/in/that house) is dangerous.

5. (I/speak/in public '在公衆場合') is difficult.

6. (The teacher/punish/so many students) seems unfair(不公平).

(E)把以下句子改爲以 *It* 開首的句子。

　例： For me to get up early is easy.

　　　It is easy for me to get up early.

1. To change a tire is easy.

2. For her to finish the job in time seems easy.

3. For me to get along with him is difficult.

4. For us to work hard is important.

5. To build such a building is a very difficult task.

(F)以 too ... to 或 enough 來改寫下列各句。

例： a.I am so busy that I can't help you.

I am *too* busy *to help* you.

b.She is so kind that she will help us.

She is kind *enough to help* us.

1. The soup is so hot that I can't drink it.

2. She spoke so fast that I couldn't understand her.

3. The teacher speaks so slowly that every student can understand her.

(提示： 要用 enough＋for＋NP＋不定詞)

4. The car is so large that it can seat(坐得下) five persons.

5. We have so much food that we can serve(供應) all our guests(客人).

6. I am so busy that I can't go to the movies with you.

(G)在以下空格中， 填入帶 to 或不帶 to 的不定詞。

例： a. He made her *tell* the truth.

b. He want *to study* hard.

1. I want my students _____ (write) a composition.

2. She made me _____ (laugh).

3. Can I help you _____ (wash) these dishes?

4. I saw three men _____ (come) out of the building.

5. She never lets me _____ (use) her new typewriter.

6. She told her daughter _____ (take) a bath.

7. We heard your dog _____ (bark '吠') loudly last night.

8. He went to the store _____ (buy) some milk.

(H)在下列各格中， 填入 to， 以代替前面已說過的不定詞， 如不需填 to 時， 則讓格子留空。

1. He likes to help others whenever he can _____.

2. Peter did not give the money although he promised _____ .

3. A: Did you close the door?

  B: No, I forgot _____ .

4. I want to write this report for you, but I don't know how _____ .

5. A: Would you like to come to our party?

  B: I'll be glad _____ .

(I)填入正確的不定詞形式(簡單式、完成式、被動式、進行式)。

1. It is important _____ (save) money.

2. I want this report _____ (type) right away.

3. I seem _____ (lose '失去') my keys.

4. The meeting is _____ (hold) next Monday.

5. They appear _____ (argue '爭論') among themselves.

(J)以不定詞或不定詞片語完成下列各句。

1. She wanted me to _____ .

2. They appear to _____ .

3. They forced him to _____ .

4. I told him not to _____ .

5. We are planning to _____ .

6. She was happy to _____ .

7. It is necessary for us to _____ .

8. She left early in order to _____ .

9. We have enough money to _____ .

10. They were too busy to _____ .

11. This box is big enough to _____ .

12. It is important to _____ .

第二十章
分詞

20.1. 分詞的種類與形式

　　分詞(participle)有**現在分詞**(present　participle)、**過去分詞**(past participle)及**完成分詞**(perfect participle)三種。其形式如下：

	主動式	被動式
現在分詞 完成分詞 過去分詞	*doing* *having done*	*being done* *having been done* *done*

　　注意：　(a)不及物動詞沒有被動式的分詞。

　　　　　(b)否定式分詞為「***not***＋**分詞**」。如 Not　having,　Not　doing anything 等。

20.2.　現在分詞

現在分詞主要用法如下：

20.2.1.　現在分詞與 be 動詞連用，構成進行時式

例如：John is walking. John 正在走路。
　　　She has been sleeping. 她一直在睡覺。
　　　（有關進行時式的細節，參看本書有關動詞時式的一章。）

20.2.2.　單字形式的現在分詞作名詞修飾語

單字形式的現在分詞置於名詞前面，作名詞的修飾語。例如：
running water 自來水　*amusing* game 有趣的遊戲
boring movie 沈悶的電影　等。

20.2.3.　片語形式的現在分詞作名詞修飾語

片語形式的現在分詞可置於名詞後面，作名詞的修飾語。例如：
1. We saw a man *standing at the corner*. 我們看到一個男人站在角落那兒。（＝We saw a man who was standing at the corner.）
2. I saw several students *waiting for the bus*. 我看到幾個學生在等公車。（＝I saw several students who were waiting

for the bus.）

20.2.4.　在 spend、come、go、there＋be ＋NP 等後面

在這些動詞及結構後面,可用現在分詞,其功能介於形容詞與副詞之間,對主詞及動詞似乎都有點修飾的意味。例如:

1. His son came *running downstairs*. 他的兒子跑著到樓下去。
2. She went *shopping yesterday*. 昨天她上街購物去。
3. I spent two hours *doing my homework*. 我花了兩小時做功課。
4. There is someone *singing outside*. 外面有人在唱歌。

20.2.5.　感官動詞、have、get、catch、find、leave 等＋受詞＋現在分詞

這些動詞的受詞後面可接現在分詞, 作受詞補語。

⑴在感官動詞 *see*、*hear*、*feel*、*smell*、*listen to*、*notice*、*watch* 等後面。

1. We *heard* the baby *crying*. 我們聽到那個嬰兒在哭。
2. I *saw* Tom *coming out from the restaurant*. 我看見 Tom 從那家餐廳出來。
3. I felt my heart *beating wildly*. 我感覺我的心在猛跳。
4. We saw the man *being attacked*. 我們看到那個男人被攻

擊。

(2)在 *have*、*get* 後面

1. I'll have Cindy *waiting for you in the office*. 我會讓 Cindy 在辦公室裏等你。

2. I won't have anyone *smoking in* my office. 我不要任何人在我的辦公室裏面抽煙。

3. He got everyone *standing up*. 他使每個人都站起來。

(3)在 *catch*、*find*、*leave* 等後面。

1. I caught him *stealing my bike*. 我捉到他偷我的車子。

2. They found her *standing by the window*. 他們發現她站在窗子旁邊。

3. We left her *waiting outside in the rain*. 我們讓她留在外面雨中等待。

20.2.6. 現在分詞可以代替子句

當兩個子句的動詞的主詞相同時，其中之一可以用分詞表示。

(1)如兩個動作同時發生，其中之一可以用現在分詞表示。例如:

1. She walked away *crying sadly*. 她傷心地哭著走了。（＝She cried sadly as she walked away.）

2. *Walking away*, she cried sadly. 她傷心地哭著走了。（＝She cried sadly as she walked away.）

(2)如動作一先一後，先者以現在分詞表示。例如:

1. ***Entering the room.*** he saw them playing chess. 他走進房間，看見他們在下棋。(＝He entered the room and then saw ... 或 After he entered the room, he saw ...)

2. ***Opening the closet,*** she took out the new dress. 她打開衣櫥，把那件新洋裝拿出來。(＝She opened the closet and then took ... 或 After she opened the closet, she took ...)

(3)現在分詞可代替 ***because/since/as*** 引導的子句。例如：

1. ***Not knowing anyone in this village,*** he felt lonesome. 因爲在這村子裏不認識任何人，他覺得很寂寞。(＝Since/Because/As he did not know anyone in this village, he felt lonesome.)

2. ***Being interested in languages,*** he decided to study linguistics. 因爲對語言感興趣，他決定唸語言學。(＝Because/Since/As he was interested in languages, he decided to study linguistics.)

20.3. 完成分詞

完成分詞的用法與上面 20.2.6.(2)之情形相同，但更明確地表示動作的先後。完成分詞強調動作完成在先。例如：

1. ***Having done his homework,*** he took a nap. 做完功課之後，他去午睡。

2. ***Having washed all the dishes,*** she went to bed. 洗完所有的盤子之後，她就去睡覺。

完成分詞最常用於按理不可能同時做的兩個動作(如「**做功課**」跟「**睡午覺**」、「**洗碗盤**」跟「**睡覺**」)，先者用完成分詞。

20.4.　過去分詞

過去分詞的用法與現在分詞相同，只是過去分詞大多數表示被動的語意。

20.4.1.　過去分詞與助動詞組合，構成完成時式及被動語態

1. She *has come*. 她已經來了。
2. The book *was written* by Thomas. 書是 Thomas 寫的。

20.4.2.　單字形式的過去分詞可置於名詞前面作修飾語(形容詞)

例如: closed doors 關閉的門

　　　broken leg 斷了的腿

　　　stolen goods 贓物(被偷的貨物)

　　　written report 書面報告

　　　crowded bus 擠滿人的公車　等。

20.4.3.　過去分詞片語可取代被動式的關係子句

例如:

1. He handed in a report **written in English**. 他交了一份用英文寫的報告。(=... a report which was written in English.)

2. Adam didn't want to drive along a road **covered with mud**.　Adam 不喜歡在一條泥濘的路上開車。(=... a road which was covered with mud.)

20.4.4.　在動詞 have、get、want、leave、find、make 等＋受詞之後

例如:

1. I want to **have** my radio **fixed**. 我想請人修理我的收音機。

2. He didn't **have** his hair **cut**. 他沒有理髮。

3. She **found** the vase **broken**. 她發現花瓶打破了。

4. He **left** his job **unfinished**. 他沒有完成他的工作。

5. He tried to **make** his ideas **understood**. 他想讓別人明白他的看法。

20.4.5.　過去分詞可以代替關係子句以外的子句

例如:

1. ***Disturbed by the loud music,*** his father turned off the radio. 因爲受那些吵鬧音樂聲所打擾, 他父親把收音機關掉。(＝His father turned off the radio because he was disturbed by the loud music.)

2. ***Frightened by the fire***, she rushd out of the room. 因爲看到火而害怕, 她就往屋外衝出去。(＝Because she was frightened by the fire, she rushed out of the room.)

20.5.　誤連分詞

　　分詞片語與不定詞片語一樣, 要注意句子主詞與分詞不能「**誤連**」, 如句子主詞與分詞不相容, 就會發生「**誤連分詞**」(misrelated participle 或 dangling participle), 其情形與不定詞一樣。(參看上面第十九章 19.7.(2)節。)例如:

1. 誤連: ****Entering*** the classroom, ***the bell*** rang. 走進教室, 鈴響了。

2. 正確: ***Entering*** the classroom, ***we*** heard ***the bell*** rang. 走進教室, 我們聽到鈴響。

　　句1的 entering 與 bell 不相容, 因爲 bell 不可能做 enter 的動作; 句2中的 entering 與 we 則相容。

3. 誤連: ****Disturbed*** by the loud music, ***the radio*** was turned off. *因爲被吵鬧的音樂所打擾, 收音機被關掉了。

4. 正確: ***Disturbed*** by the loud music, ***his father*** turned off the radio. 因爲被吵鬧的音樂所打擾, 他爸爸把收音機關掉了。

20.6. 獨立分詞結構

　　上面幾節所說的分詞片語中，分詞的主詞與句子的主詞均指同一人或物，因此分詞片語中都不必表示其「**主詞**」。但若分詞的「**主詞**」與句子的主詞不同時，分詞的「**主詞**」(亦即"做"分詞動作的人或物)就要表示出來。帶有分詞的主事者名詞的分詞片語稱爲「**獨立分詞結構**」(absolute participle construction)。例如：

1. ***The weather being fine,*** we decided to go jogging. (因爲)天氣好，我們決定去慢跑。
2. ***Her mother being away,*** she had to take care of her little brother. (因爲)母親外出，她必須照顧她弟弟。
3. She is walking along slowly, ***her baby held tightly in her arms.*** 她慢慢地走，把嬰兒緊抱著。

《習題 24》

(A)將下列各句改爲含現在分詞的句子。

　例：I saw a man who was standing at the corner.

　　　→ I saw a man *standing* at the corner.

1. The man who is standing there is my brother.
2. The man who is walking across the street is his father-in-law.
3. We saw a dog which is chasing a cat along the street.
4. The boy who was trying to catch the bus was hit by a motorcycle.
5. The woman who is now putting bandage(繃帶) on Tom's hand is a

nurse.

(B)將下列各句改寫爲含有過去分詞的句子。

  例： The girl who was hit by a motorcycle was Edward's sister.

    → The girl *hit* by a motorcycle was Edward's sister.

1. The boy who was rescued(救) by the lifeguard(救生員) did not know how to swim.

2. I know the boy who was bitten by our dog.

3. The money which was stolen from my store was found by the police.

4. I have just received a package(包裹) which was sent to me by airmail.

5. The girl who was dressed in red was a student of Dr. Johnson's.

6. The music which is being played now is written by Chopin(蕭邦).

7. The boy who is being examined by the doctor looks a little pale(蒼白).

(C)將下列各句改寫爲含有分詞的句子。

  例： a. When he entered the room, he saw Jane crying.→ *Entering the room, he saw Jane crying.*

    b. Because he was encouraged(鼓勵) by his teacher, he decided to major(主修) in physics(物理).→ *Encouraged by his teacher, he decided to major in physics.*

1. After she opened the door, she saw Peter in the room reading a magazine.

2. Since he did not know anyone in class, the new student felt quite helpless(無助的).

3. After he had made up his mind, he quitted his job. (提示：用完成分詞)

4. Because he is interested in language, he plans to become an interpreter (口譯員).

5. When they enter the house, they found a thief in the living room.

第二十一章
動名詞

21.1. 動名詞的形式

動名詞(gerund)的形式與現在分詞及完成分詞相同, 例如 writing、having written、being written、having been written 等。

動名詞是當作名詞而使用的 V-*ing* 形式。

21.2. 動名詞的用法

21.2.1. 動名詞作句子主詞

例如:

1. *Studying English* can be fun. 唸英文可以是有趣的。
2. *Listening to popular music* bored him. 聽流行音樂使他覺得無聊。

3. ***Tom's smoking in the office*** disturbed almost everyone there. Tom 在辦公室內抽烟使在那裏的每一個人幾乎都覺得不安。

4. ***Swimming*** is her favorite sport. 游泳是她喜愛的運動。

另外，動名詞也常用於表示禁止某種活動的簡短標語，如 ***No parking*** 「不准停車」、***No smoking*** 「禁止抽烟」等。

21.2.2.　動名詞作句子受詞

例如：

1. He doesn't like ***swimming***. 他不喜歡游泳。

2. She has just finished ***doing her homework***. 她剛做完功課。

3. We must avoid ***over-eating***. 我們必須避免吃得太多。

21.2.3.　動名詞作主詞補語

動名詞可置於 be 動詞後面，作主詞補語。例如：

1. His favorite sport　is ***swimming***. 他喜愛的運動是游泳。

2. My first job was ***selling sewing machines***. 我第一份工作是賣縫紉機。

3. One of her hobbies is ***collecting stamps***. 她的嗜好之一是集郵。

21.2.4.　動名詞作介詞受詞

動名詞可置於介詞後面，作介詞的受詞。例如：

1. She is tired *of doing her homework.* 她做功課做得厭煩了。
2. I am sorry *for not helping you.* 我很抱歉沒有幫你的忙。
3. She is thinking *of buying a new car.* 她正在考慮要買一部新汽車。
4. He is afraid *of being punished.* 他怕受處罰。
5. I am fond *of grass skiing.* 我喜歡滑草。
6. There is no point *in arguing with him*. 跟他爭論沒有用處。
7. The nurse is responsible *for taking care of the baby.* 這護士負責照顧這嬰兒。

21.2.5. 動名詞作名詞同位語

動名詞可以像名詞一樣,當作另外一個名詞的同位語。注意逗號的使用。例如:

1. His plan, *building a 30-story building,* is considered to be impractical. 他的計劃, 也就是要建一幢 30 層的大樓, 被認為不切實際。
2. Her recent study, *analyzing the use of gerund,* takes up a lot of her time. 她最近的研究, 也就是分析動名詞的用法, 佔用了她很多的時間。

21.3. 動詞與動名詞連用

在第十九章中, 我們學到不定詞可以作動詞的受詞,上面 19.2.2.節中我

們也說過，動名詞也可以作動詞的受詞。因此，我們會問，是不是所有動詞後面都可以接動名詞或不定詞呢？答案是否定的。

一般說來，有三種情形：

　　a.有些動詞後面只能接動名詞，不能接不定詞。

　　b.有些動詞後面可接動名詞或不定詞，其語意完全沒有或沒有多大的差異。

　　c.有些動詞後面可接動名詞或不定詞，但二者之意義有所不同。

以下分別討論這三種情形。

21.3.1.

有些動詞後面可接動名詞，或其他結構(如 that 子句)，但是不能接不定詞。這類動詞常用的有：

admit　承認	avoid　避免
appreciate　欣賞/感謝	consider　考慮
delay　延遲	deny　否認
dislike　不喜歡	endure　忍受
enjoy　喜歡/覺得高興	escape　逃避
excuse　原諒	face　面對
feel like　很想	finish　完成
forgive　原諒	give up　放棄
imagine　想像	can't help　禁不住/不能不
keep　保持/一直不斷	can't stand　不能忍受
mention　提及	miss　錯過
mind　介意(主要用於否定及疑問句)	risk　冒險

| practice | 練習 | | suggest | 提議 | 等。 |
| understand | 明白 | | | | |

另外，有些常用說法後面也接動名詞。例如：

it's no good/use V-ing	做…沒有用
there's no point in V-ing	做…沒有用
it's worth V-ing	做…是值得的
to have difficulty V-ing	做…有困難
spend time V-ing	花時間做…
waste time V-ing	浪費時間做…

以上說法的解釋中「**做…**」表示做動名詞 V-ing 的動作。

例如：

1. She keeps *complaining about the noise upstairs.* 她一直不斷抱怨樓上的噪音。

2. Would you mind *opening the window*? 請你把窗子打開？

3. I don't mind *helping her.* 我不介意幫助她。

4. This film is *worth seeing.* 這部片子值得看。

5. It's no use *trying to apologize to him.* 跟他道歉是沒用的。

6. He spent two hours *fixing the radio.* 他花了兩小時來修理這個收音機。

21.3.2.

有些動詞後面可以接動名詞或不定詞，其語意完全沒有差異或沒有多大差異。這類動詞常用的有：

| advise | 建議 | allow | 允許 |
| begin | 開始 | can't bear | 不能忍受 |

cease　停止	continue　繼續
intend　打算	recommend　推薦
permit　允許	require　需要
start　開始	want　需要
like　喜歡	love　喜愛
hate　很不喜歡	prefer　比較喜歡　等。

例如:

1. We began *to shout.* 我們開始大叫。

   We began *shouting.*

2. I like *to help him.* 我喜歡幫助他。

   I like *helping him.*

3. They intend *to sell the house.* 他們打算把房子出售。

   They intend *selling the house.*

4. I prefer *parking here.*　我比較喜歡在這兒停車。

   I prefer *to park here.*

21.3.3.

有些動詞後面可以接動名詞或不定詞, 但其語意不同。分別說明如下:

⑴動詞 *remember* '記得'、*forget* '忘記'、*regret* '後悔'、*stop* '停止'、*go on* '繼續' 後面接動名詞時, 動名詞表示較早(比較這些動詞更早)發生的動作。但與不定詞連用時, 不定詞的動作在動詞的動作之後才發生。例如:

1. I *remember seeing* him at the library. 我記得在圖書館看見他。(see 在 remember 之前)

2. I *remembered to lock* the door. 我(當時)記得把門上鎖。(lock 在 remember 之後)

3. She *stopped talking* to me. 她停止跟我說話。(talk 在先, stop 在後; 句意是'她一直在跟我說話, 然後就停下來不再說了'。)

4. She *stopped to ask* me a question. 她停了下來, 要問我一個問題。(stop 在先, ask 在後)

5. I *forget giving* her my address. 我忘記給過她我的地址。(give 在先, forget 在後; 句意是'我把地址給了她了, 只是我忘了這件事'。)

6. I *forget to give* her my address. 我忘記把我的地址給她。(forget 在先, give 在後; 事實上因爲'忘記'的緣故, 所以也沒有把地址給她。)

(2)「動詞 *see*、*watch*、*hear* ＋動名詞」表示看/聽到動名詞動作的一部分(我們看/聽到這動作時, 動作本身正在進行中)。例如:

1. I *heard* him *practicing* the piano. 我聽見他正在練習鋼琴。

但「*see*、*watch*、*hear* ＋不帶 *to* 不定詞」則表示看/聽到不定詞動作的全部過程。例如:

2. I *heard* her *play* that sonata. 我聽到她彈奏了那首奏鳴曲。(暗示我聽到整首曲子, 她從頭到尾彈奏的過程。)

(3)「*be sorry* ＋不定詞」表示爲正在做或將要做的事情表示歉意。例如:

1. I am *sorry to disturb* you. 我很抱歉, 要打擾你了。

但「*be sorry* ＋動名詞」則表示爲早先所做過的事抱歉。例如:

2. I am *sorry for waking* you *up* so early this morning. 我

很抱歉，今天早上那麼早就把你給弄醒了。

21.4. 動名詞用法上應注意的一些事項

⑴如動名詞緊接於動詞後面時，句子的主詞也就是做動名詞動作的人。例如：

1. I *don't like smoking* in the office. 我不喜歡在辦公室裏抽烟。（抽烟的人是‘我’）

但如果動名詞與動詞之間有所有格形容詞(如 *his, my, her, their* 等)或受格代名詞(如 *him, her, them*)時，做動名詞動作的人是所有格形容詞或受格代名詞所指的人。例如

2. I *don't like his/him smoking* in the office. 我不喜歡他在辦公室抽烟。（抽烟的人是‘他’）

其他的例子有：*dislike* ‘不喜歡’、*insist on* ‘堅持’、*mind* ‘介意’、*propose* ‘提議’、*stop* ‘制止’、*suggest* ‘建議’、*object to* ‘反對’ 等。例如：

3. He *objects to my/me helping* her. 他反對我幫助他。（‘我’ 幫助她）

4. He *objects to helping* her. 他反對幫助她。（‘他’ 幫助她）

⑵動名詞的完成式是「*having*＋過去分詞」。被動式是「*being*＋過去分詞」／「*having been*＋過去分詞」。否定式爲「*not*＋動名詞」。例如：

1. She was accused of *having stolen* my money. 她被指控偷了我的錢。

2. I don't like *being punished.* 我不喜歡被懲罰。

3. I am sorry for **not helping** you. 我很抱歉沒有幫助你。

(3) **Mind** 主要用於否定句及疑問句，後面可接動名詞，但不能接不定詞。例如：

1. Do you mind **waiting for me**? 你可以等我嗎？
2. I don't mind **going to bed early tonight**. 我不介意今晚早睡。

(4)含有介詞 to 的片語後面要用動名詞。這些片語常用者如 **be used to** '習慣於'、**be accustomed to** '習慣於'、**look forward to** '企盼/期望/盼望' 等。例如：

1. I **am looking forward to seeing** you soon. 我盼望不久可以見到你。(不可以說：*... forward to see ...)
2. I **am used to living in** the city. 我習慣住在城市裏。(不可以說：*... used to live ...)

《習題25》

(A)以下各句中，使用主動或被動的動名詞。

　例：a. He likes *sitting* on that sofa.

　　　b. He doesn't like *being punished*.

1. _____ (Be)honest is advisable.
2. I am not interested in _____ (study)English.
3. She does not like _____ (take)to the hospital.
4. We must avoid _____ (eat)too much.

5. She enjoys _____ (shop) at the supermarket.

6. _____ (Smoke) is not allowed here.

7. It is no use _____ (try) to help them.

8. I can't stand _____ (tell) what to do.

9. They are used to _____ (live) on the ground floor.

10. He was punished for _____ (not hand in) his homework on time.

(B) 以動名詞完成下列各句。注意主動及被動式。

例： a. _____ (swim) in the ocean can be dangerous.

　　　Swimming in the ocean can be dangerous.

　　b. He doesn't like _____ (laugh at) by other people.

　　He doesn't like being laughed at by other people.

1. She enjoys _____ (drive) at night.

2. I have just finished _____ (wash) the car.

3. _____ (Help) him to wax the floor will make me very tired.

4. _____ (Criticize '批評') by his teacher hurts his feelings.

5. I blamed the maid for _____ (not clean) the kitchen.

6. We try our best to avoid _____ (spend) too much money.

7. He can't stand _____ (punish) by the teacher.

8. She is responsible for _____ (take) care of her baby sister.

9. We look forward to _____ (see) you next Monday.

10. I enjoy _____ (play) basketball.

(C) 選擇正確的形式。

1. I enjoy (being, to be, be) alone.

2. I would like (buying, to buy) a pair of new shoes for Joe.

3. The book is worth (to read, read, reading).

4. If he did not hand in his homework, he would risk '冒險' (to be punished, being punished) by his teacher.

5. We are looking forward to(watch, watching) him(play, to play) the game.

6. Would you want me(say, to say, saying) it again?

7. Please remember(to give, giving, give) me a call when you arrive.

8. I remember(to see, see, seeing) him at the library the other day.

9. I told him not to forget(saying, to say) "Thank you."

10. I would like to fish, but they did not allow(to fish, fishing) here.

第二十二章
關係子句

22.1. 認識關係子句

「關係子句」(relative clause)又稱為「形容詞子句」(adjective clause)，因為其功能與形容詞相同，修飾名詞。例如:

1. Do you know the boy *who gave me this book*? 你認識那個給我這本書的男孩嗎?

2. This is the book *that I bought at the sale*. 這是我在減價時買的書。

在1、2兩句中，斜體部分都是關係子句，who 所引導的子句修飾 the boy; that 所引導的子句修飾 the book。

含關係子句的句子可以看作是兩個句子的組合，例句1與2可以分析成例句3與4。

3. a. Do you know *the boy*?

   b. *The boy* gave me this book.

4. a. This is *the book*.

   b. I bought *the book* at the sale.

　　3 a 與 3 b 中的 the boy 指同一人，而 4 a 與 4 b 中的 the book 指同一本書。按關係子句形成法則，以關係代名詞取代指稱相同的名詞中後面的一個，成爲關係子句與主要子句組合成一個「**複合句**」(complex sentence)，而關係代名詞前面的名詞則稱爲關係代名詞的「**先行詞**」(antecedent)。

　　因此，在例句 1 裏，who 是關係代名詞，the boy 是先行詞。在例句 2 裏，that 是關係代名詞，the book 是先行詞。

　　同時，從例句 3 與 4 的分析中，我們可以知道，關係代名詞除了引導關係子句以外，本身亦在關係子句中具有名詞的功能。例如例句 1 中的 who 是關係子句動詞 gave 的主詞(從 3 b 可知)，即例句 2 中的 that 是關係子句動詞 bought 的受詞(從 4 b 可知)。

　　關係代名詞既能引導從屬子句，又兼具子句中名詞的功能。這種特性與純粹引導子句的連接詞(如 because, since, although 等)不同，因此，很多文法書都把關係代名詞引導的關係子句當作特別的一種子句來介紹。

22.2.　常用的關係子句

　　關係子句可依其先行詞及引導句的「**關係詞**」(relative words，包括關係代名詞 who、that 等以及關係副詞如 when、where 等)來分類。常用的種類如下：

先行詞	關係詞	例　　　　　　　　　　句
指人	關係代名詞： *who, whom* *whose, that*	關係詞在關係子句中的功能： 主詞：I know the ***boy who/that*** gave me the book. 受詞：He liked the ***secretary who/whom/that*** he had hired. 介詞受詞：The ***boy to whom*** she spoke was her cousin. 所有格形容詞：This is the ***man whose*** picture you just saw. 補語：She is not the ***type of person that/which*** your cousin is. (比較不常用)
指物	關係代名詞： *which, that*	關係詞在關係子中的功能： 主詞：This is the book ***which/that*** describes Africa. 受詞：This is the book ***which/that*** I bought yesterday. 介詞受詞：This is the ***table under which*** the boy sat. 補語：This is the ***type of car which*** my own is not. (比較不常用)
指時間 指地方 指理由	關係副詞： *when* *where* *why*	That was the ***day when*** she got married. This is the ***house where*** I was born. Give me a good ***reason why*** you are late.

22.3. 關係子句的引導詞

22.3.1. 關係代名詞

⑴關係代名詞與其先行詞在文法的「**性**」與「**數**」的形式上要一致:

(A)性:

先行詞	關係代名詞
人	*who* (如 the boy who ...)
(非人)事、物	*which* (如 the table which ...)
	注意: *that* 的先行詞人或事、物均可。

(B)數:

先行詞	關係代名詞
the *boy*	*who is ...*
the *boys*	*who are ...*

⑵關係代名詞的「**格**」取決於其在關係子句中的文法功能。如關係代名詞在關係子句中作主詞或補語,則是「**主格**」; 如作受詞或介詞受詞,則是「**受格**」; 如作所有格形容詞,則是「**所有格**」。例如:

the boy *who* gave me the book (主格)

the boy *who*(*whom*) he hired (受格)

the boy to *whom* she speaks (受格)

the boy *whose* father is a lawyer (所有格)

(3)常用的關係代名詞有：*who*、*whom*、*whose*、*which*、*that*。其用法如下：

(A) *who*、*whom*、與 *whose*

who、whom、whose 指人；*whose* 除指人以外，也可以指事物。

(a)作關係子句主詞時用 *who*。例如：

1. The man *who stole your money* was arrested. 偷了你的錢的那個人被捕了。

2. The girl *who is standing by the piano* is my cousin. 站在鋼琴旁邊的那個女孩子是我的表妹(姐)。

(b)作關係子句受詞時用 *who* 或 *whom*; 作介詞受詞時用 *whom*。例如：

1. He likes the secretary *who*(或 *whom*) *he has just hired.* 他喜歡那個他剛雇用的秘書。(**注意**：在現代英語中 whom 是很正式的用法，平常大多用 who)

2. The man *to whom I spoke* was an English teacher. 我跟他談話的那個人是一位英語老師。(**注意**：如介詞 to 不移前，仍置於 spoke 後面，則常可用 who 取代 whom。如：The man *who I spoke to* was ....)

(c)作受詞之 *who*/*whom* 可以省略。例如：

1. a. He likes the secretary *who*(*m*) *he has just hired.* 他喜歡那位他剛雇用的秘書。

   b. He likes the secretary *he has just hired.* (a、b 兩句語

意一樣)

2. a. The man *who*(*m*) *I spoke to* is an English teacher. 我
跟他說話的那個人是一位英語老師。

b. The man *I spoke to* is an English teacher.(a、b 兩句語
意一樣)

注意: 如介詞在關係代名詞之前時, 如 *to whom*、*for whom* 等關係
代名詞不可省略。

(d)代替關係子句中含所有格的詞組時, 用 *whose*。例如

1. The woman *whose son you just met* is Mrs. Johnson. 你
剛才遇見她的兒子的那個女人是 Johnson 太太。(＝那個女人是
Johnson 太太, 你剛才遇見她的兒子。)

2. The girl *whose sister is our secretary* is very pretty. 她
的妹妹是我們的秘書的那個女孩子很漂亮。(＝那個女孩子很漂
亮, 她的妹妹是我們的秘書。)

例句 1 與 2 是由例句 3 與 4 的兩對句子分別合併組成。

3. *The woman* is Mrs. Johnson.

You just met *the woman's* son.

4. *The girl* is very pretty.

The girl's sister is our secretary.

whose 也可以用於事物。例如:

5. The book *whose cover is green* is very expensive. 封面是
綠色的那本書很貴。

(B) *which*

(a) *which* 主要指動物或事、物。其主格及受格形式都一樣。例如：

1. He doesn't like the shirt *which he bought yesterday.* 他不喜歡那件他昨天買的襯衫。

2. The book *which is on the desk* belongs to Tim. 在桌子上的那本書屬於 Tim 的。

3. The table *on which he is standing* is very small. 他站在上面的那張桌子很小。

(b)作受詞用的 *which* 可以省略。例如：

1. He doesn't like the shirt *he bought* yesterday.

2. The table *he is standing on* is very small.

(c)指事物之所有格的名詞組時，可以用 *whose*，如上面(A)(d)之例句 5。但正式用法用 *of which*。例如：

1. The book *whose cover is green* is expensive.

2. The book *the cover of which is green* is expensive. 封面是綠色的那本書很貴。

注意：例 2 這種用法非常正式，現代英語中並不常用。

(d) *which* 可指前述的整個句子。例如：

1. She said she was rich, *which was not true.* 她說她很有錢，(但)這不是真實的。(which 指 she was rich 這件事。)

2. He is always late, *which makes his teacher very angry.* 他老是遲到，這使他的老師非常生氣。(which 指 he is always late 這件事。)

(C) *that*

(a) *that* 可指人或事、物，作主詞或受詞均可。但作介詞受詞時，that 不能置於介詞後面。例如：

1. The man *that stole my money* was arrested. 偷我錢的那個男人被捕了。(主詞)

2. I like the pen *that you bought yesterday.* 我喜歡你昨天買的那支筆。(受詞)

3. The man *that I spoke to* is a history teacher. 我跟他說話的那個人是一位歷史老師。(介詞 to 的受詞；但**注意**：不可以說 *The man to that I spoke ....)

(b)作受詞的 *that* 可以省略。例如：

1. I like the pen *you bought yesterday.* 我喜歡你昨天買的那支筆。

2. The man *I spoke to* is a history teacher, 我跟他說話的那個人是一位歷史老師。

(c)先行詞含有 *the same*、*the only*、*the first*、*the best*、*the next*、*all* 等修飾語；或先行詞為 *anything*、*all*、*everything*、*nothing*、*little*、*much* 等不定代名詞時，通常關係代名詞用 *that* 而不用 *which*。例如：

1. He is *the best teacher that* we have ever had. 他是我們所有過的最好的好師。

2. She was *the only one that* came to the party. 她是來聚會的唯一的人。

3. ***Anything that*** you say will be helpful to us. 你所說的任何事情都會對我們有所幫助。

(d)如有兩個先行詞，一指人另一指物時，先行詞用 ***that***。例如：

She told us about all the ***interesting people*** and ***the old buildings that*** she saw in Europe. 她把她在歐洲看到的所有有趣的人物以及古老的建築告訴我們。

22.3.2.　關係副詞

⑴關係副詞有 ***where***、***when***、***why*** 三個，分別與表示地方、時間、理由/原因之副詞組相對應。例如：

1. a. This is ***the house.***
   b. She was born ***in the house.***
   → This is the house ***where*** he was born. 這是他在那兒出生的房子。

2. a. That was ***the year.***
   b. Our school was founded ***in the year.***
   → That was the year ***when*** our school was founded. 那是我們學校成立的一年。

3. a. That was ***the reason.***
   b. She was late ***for the reason.***
   → That was the reason ***why*** she was late. 那是她為什麼遲到的理由。

關係副詞可以用「**介詞＋關係代名詞**」取代。例如：

4. This is the house ***in which*** I was born.

5. That was the year *in which* our school was founded.

6. That was the reason *for which* she was late.

例 4、5、6 的語意與 1、2、3 相同，只是 4、5、6 比較正式；而且以 *for which* 代替 *why* 的合文法程度還有所爭議，有些文法學家認為合文法(如 Thomson & Martinet 1986, p.83)，但有些則認為其被接受的程度不高 (如 Quirk 等人，1985，p.1254)。因此，初學者宜避免使用。

⑵很多人認為 *the year when*、*the place where*，特別是 *the reason why* 等說法在語意上有些重複，因此會把語意上多餘的先行詞省略。例如：

1. This is *where I was born*. 這是我在那兒出生的地方。

2. That was *when our school was founded*. 那是我們學校成立的一年。

3. That was *why she was late*. 那是她遲到的理由。

⑶表示時間及理由之關係副詞 *when* 及 *why* 可以省略；但表示地方的關係副詞 *where* 若省略時，要保留介詞。例如：

1. This is *the year* our school was founded. 那是我們學校成立的一年。

2. That was *the reason* she was late. 那是她遲到的理由。

3. This is *the house* I was born *in*. 這是我在那兒出生的房子。

22.4. 限制關係子句與非限制關係子句

⑴「限制關係子句」(restrictive relative clauses)對其先行詞加以特別

的描述與界定，使其先行詞與其同類之人或事物有所區別。例如：

1. The man *who lives next door* is my best friend. 住在隔壁的那個男人是我最要好的朋友。

例句1的關係子句在所有的 "man" 當中，限定了其中的一個，亦即是住在隔壁的那個，而不是任何一個。由於有這種功能，我們稱這種關係子句為「**限制關係子句**」。

(2)「**非限制關係子句**」(non-restrictive relative clauses)置於本身已有特指或已經被界定的先行詞之後，提供有關這先行詞更多的資訊。例如：

2. Jane, *who has been singing loudly,* is my neighbor. Jane 是我的鄰居，她一直在大聲唱歌。

注意：　(a)非限制關係子句要用**逗點**(comma)與主要子句分開。

　　　　(b)例句2中的 Jane 已經是指特別的某一個人，並非任何人。因此，說話者不必特別界定哪一個 Jane。關係子句所提供的，只是有關 Jane 的一些額外的訊息而已。

(3)限制與非限制關係子句的語意有如上面(1)與(2)所述。有時候，這種差別會很大。例如：

1. Her son *who lives in New York* calls her up every week. 她住在紐約的兒子每星期都打電話給她。

2. Her son, *who lives in New York,* calls her up every week. 她的兒子住在紐約，他每星期都打電話給她。

例句1的 who 子句是限制關係子句，告訴我們她不止一個兒子，其中住在紐約的那個兒子每週打電話給她，其他的兒子可能並不如此。

例句2的 who 子句是非限制關係子句，並沒在其先行詞的同類中指定或界定其一，也不具有「**她不止有一個兒子**」的含義。因此，她非常可能只有

一個兒子，而這兒子住在紐約。

　　所以，對於通常「只有一個」的人或事物，如要用關係子句來修飾時，只能用非限定關係子句。

　　⑷非限定關係子句也可以用來修飾事、物。例如：

　　The 7:30 train, *which is usually very punctual,* was late this morning. 七點三十分的那班火車今天早上來遲了，這班車通常是準時的。

注意： ⑷非限制關係子句的關係代名詞不用 that。

　　　　⑸非限制關係子句在體裁上比較正式。

22.5.　all、both、few、most、several、some、one、two、three 等＋of＋ $\left\{\begin{array}{l} \text{which} \\ \text{whom} \end{array}\right\}$

　　在非限制關係子句中，我們可以用下面句式，來指先行詞中的全部或一部分。先行詞必須是複數，人、物皆可。

…先行詞, $\left\{\begin{array}{l} \textbf{\textit{all}} \\ \textbf{\textit{both}} \\ \vdots \end{array}\right\}$ 等＋of＋ $\left\{\begin{array}{l} \text{which} \\ \text{whom} \end{array}\right\}$ …

1. I have fifty students, *twenty of whom* failed in the mid-term exam. 我有五十個學生，其中二十個期中考試不及格。

2. She bought a dozen apples, *several of which* were badly bruised. 她買了一打蘋果，其中有幾個碰損得很厲害。

《習題 26》

(A)在以下各題中，將 b 部分改成關係子句，填入 a 部分之空格裏，使成為一個複合句。

例：
- a. I know the man ＿＿＿＿＿.
- b. The man came here yesterday.

→ *I know the man who came here yesterday.*

1.
- a. The police arrested the man ＿＿＿＿＿.
- b. The man stole my money.

2.
- a. The girl ＿＿＿＿＿came to the office very late this morning.
- b. The company recently(最近) hired the girl.

3.
- a. We heard the good news ＿＿＿＿＿.
- b. We were expecting the good news.

4.
- a. Baseball, ＿＿＿＿＿, is a popular sport in Taiwan.
- b. I know nothing about baseball.

5.
- a. Chinese painting, ＿＿＿＿＿, is a form of art.
- b. Many people do not understand Chinese painting.

6.
- a. This house, ＿＿＿＿＿, belongs to John.
- b. This house was built in 1915.

7.
- a. The policeman stopped the car ＿＿＿＿＿.
- b. The car had gone through the red light(闖紅燈).

8.
- a. The man ＿＿＿＿＿did not say anything to the police.
- b. The man's money had been stolen.

9.
- a. The man ＿＿＿＿＿is our new teacher.
- b. Mary is talking to the man.

10. {
a. The new English teacher, _____, is Mary's cousis.
b. The new English teacher is very young.
}

(B)以下各對句子中，將其中一項改爲「非限制關係子句」，再將兩句合併爲一句。注意逗點的使用。

例： {
a. Tom goes to school everyday.
Tom is a junor high school student.
}

→ Tom, *who is a junior high school student,* goes to school every-day.

{
b. We all like Alice.
Alice is our English teacher.
}

→ We all like Alice, *who is our English teacher.*

1. {
Mary introduced me to her son.
Her son is a police officer.
}

2. {
My boss was late this morning.
My boss usually comes to work on time.
}

3. {
Peter's mother goes jogging everyday.
Peter's mother is 45 years old.
}

4. {
We are going to go to Hong Kong.
Our uncle lives in Hong Kong.
}

5. {
I will see Dr. Wang.
Dr. Wang has been our family doctor for many years.
}

6. {
The young man is the best basketball player in our school team.
I don't remember the young man's name.
}

7. {
Jane did not come to my party.
Jane is my best friend.
}

8. $\begin{cases} \text{He went to Hsin-chu.} \\ \text{Hsin-chu is only 60 kilometer away from here.} \end{cases}$

(C)填入適當的關係代名詞。

1. Do you know the boy _____ is standing over there?

2. I will give you everything _____ you want.

3. The student _____ you saw yesterday is one of Dr. Wang's assistants.

4. Tom was the only boy _____ can answer this question.

5. They always blame her for everything _____ goes wrong.

6. The movie is the worst movie _____ I have ever seen.

7. Cindy is the girl _____ grade is the highest in the class.

8. This is the novel(小説) about _____ we have been talking.

9. Bob is the only person _____ cares about me.

10. This story is about a girl _____ father is a millionaire.

(D)用關係副詞 where, when 或 why 來合併以下各對句子。

例: $\begin{cases} \text{This is the house.} \\ \text{He was born in the house.} \end{cases}$

→ This is the house *where* he was born.

1. $\begin{cases} \text{Last Sunday was the day.} \\ \text{We had our party on that day.} \end{cases}$

2. $\begin{cases} \text{This is the place.} \\ \text{The money might be kept in this place.} \end{cases}$

3. $\begin{cases} \text{I know the reason.} \\ \text{You bought the car for that reason.} \end{cases}$

4. { Can you tell me the time?
    Mr. Sandos arrives at that time.

5. { We will never know the reason.
    He left town for that reason.

6. { I am going to stay at that hotel.
    I can have a lot of privacy at that hotel.

7. { I was born in the year.
    We won the war in that year.

8. { Winter is the season.
    A lot of people go skiing in that season.

(E)以 all、both …等＋of＋which 或 whom 來合併下列各對句子。

例： { He gave me some books.
      Two of them have red covers.

　　→ He gave me some books, *two of which* have red covers.

1. { She gave me thirty books.
    Some of them were very expensive.

2. { I have a lot of friends.
    All of them have cars.

3. { She has two brothers.
    One of them is six feet tall.

4. { She sent me two letters.
    One of them was very short.

5. { She gave me a lot of information.
    Most of it was useless.

(F)仿照例句，在以下各句後面加上一個含有意指整個主要子句的句意的 which 所引

導的關係子句。

例：I was absent yesterday, *which made my teacher very angry.*

1. I didn't go to Shirley's party,_____.

2. John is still using the phone,_____.

3. She came home very late,_____.

4. They lost their bicycles,_____.

5. They didn't like our plan,_____.

6. We did a good job,_____.

7. The weather was not good yesterday,_____.

第二十三章
連接詞與子句

23.1. 連接詞簡說

「連接詞」(conjunctions)與介詞相似，都是沒有詞尾或其他字形變化的字。其功能是連接兩個子句，使成為一個句子。

連接詞分為兩大類：(1)「對等連接詞」(coordinating conjunction)如 *and*、*or*、*but*、*so* 等；(2)「從屬連接詞」(subordinating conjunction)如 *because*、*lf*、*when*、*though*、*that*、*which*、*where*、*after*、*before* 等。

23.2. 對等連接、從屬連接、子句

23.2.1. 對等連接與對等子句

「對等連接」是利用對等連接詞把兩個功能相當的結構連接在一起(例如

名詞與名詞、動詞與動詞、片語與片語、子句與子句)。連接以後，被連接的兩個結構的文法功能依舊是相當獨立對等，並無主從之分。

如對等連接詞連接的是兩個子句，則兩個子句都稱爲「對等子句」(coordinate clauses)。

我們以下面的圖解，說明對等連接的情形。

1. I saw *Mary and Tom*. 我看見 Mary 和 Tom。(and 連接兩個名詞)

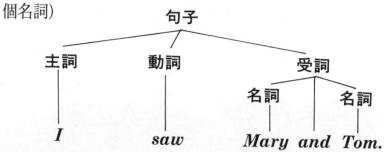

句1的 Tom 與 Mary 以 *and* 來連接，兩者之文法功能對等，圖中以併立的方式表示。

2. I like your hair style *but* Tom likes your dress. 我喜歡你的髮型但是 Tom 喜歡你的洋裝。

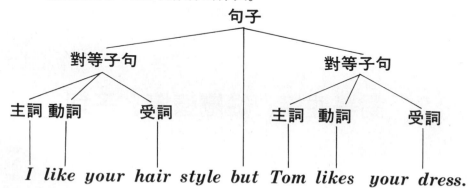

句2的兩個子句以 *but* 來連接，兩者的功能也是對等，並無主從之分，在圖中也是以併立的方式表示。這種由對等子句組成的句子也稱爲「併合句」

(compound sentence)。

23.2.2.　從屬連接與主要子句及從屬子句

從屬連接是利用從屬連接詞把兩個子句連接在一起。連接以後，以連接詞所引導的子句變成另一子句的一部分稱爲「**從屬子句**」(subordinate clause)，而另一子句則稱爲「**主要子句**」(main clause)。

我們以以下圖解來說明從屬連接的情形。

1. He said *that* he saw me. 他說他看見我。

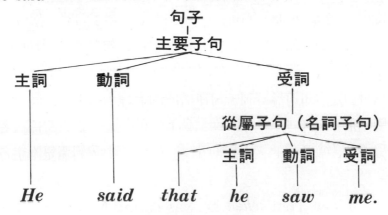

從上面圖中，我們可以清楚地看見，that 引導的子句只是主要子句的一部分，做主要子句中動詞 said 的受詞。因此，這種句子稱爲「**從屬子句**」。而依其文法功能來分類，以上例 1 的從屬子句稱爲「**名詞子句**」(noun clause)。除名詞子句以外，從屬子句還有「**形容詞子句**」(adjective clause)與「**副詞子句**」(adverb clause)兩大類。

含有從屬子句的句子稱爲「**複合句**」(complex sentence)。以下我們以例句 2、3 來分別說明形容詞子句及副詞子句的功能與結構。

2. He saw the man *who*(*m*)Tom admired. 他看見 Tom 欽佩的那個人。

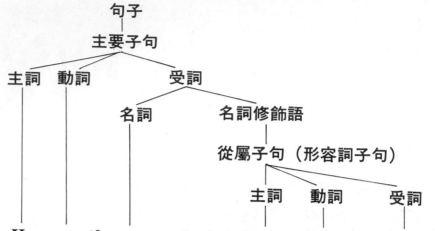

He saw the man who(m) Tom admired (the man).

從屬子句 *who*(*m*) Tom admired 是主要子句的一部分, 故主要子句受詞 the man 的修飾語, 因此稱爲「**形容詞子句**」(亦即「**關係子句**」, 見前面第二十二章)。

另外, 我們知道形容詞子句在構成的過程中, 其中必有一個名詞是主要及從屬兩個子句中所共有的, 而這個共有的詞組, 就由關係代名詞表示, 而在從屬子句中就不必再說(或寫)出來。但圖解中我們還是附上, 使句子的結構更清楚。

3. I saw Tom *when* he was eating his lunch. 我在 Tom 吃午飯時看見他。

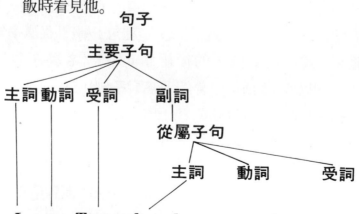

I saw Tom when he was eating his lunch.

以上圖解也顯示出 *when* 所引導的子句構成主要子句的一部分，做主要子句動詞 saw 的修飾語，功能爲時間副詞，因此也稱爲「副詞子句」。

23.3. 對等連接詞

對等連接詞形態上有三種：⑴**單字形**，如 *and*、*or*、*but*、*so*、*for*、*nor*、*yet*、*still* 等；⑵**對稱形**，如 *either ... or*、*neither ...nor*、*not only ... but also*、*both ... and* 等；⑶**片語形**，如 *as well as*、*no less than*、*rather than* 等。

⑴ *and* 與 *both ... and*

1. We need some paper *and* a pen. 我們需要一些紙和一枝筆。
2. The dictionary is very good *and* it sells very well. 這本字典很好，而且也很暢銷。
3. *Both* Betty *and* Clara are here. Betty 和 Clara 兩人都在這兒。
4. The story is *both* exciting *and* interesting. 這個故事旣緊張又有趣。

⑵ *or* 與 *either or*

1. Did you see a boy *or* a girl? 你看見一個男孩子或是一個女孩子呢？
2. You must come home early,*or* your mother will be angry with you. 你必須早點回家，否則你媽媽會生氣。
3. *Either* you *or* she is responsible for this. 你或是她要爲此

事負責。

　4. I did not pass the test. **Either** the questions are too difficult, **or** I did not work hard enough. 我沒有通過這個測驗。要嘛是題目太難，要嘛就是我不夠用功。

⑶ **nor** 及 **neither** ... **nor**

　1. I saw **neither** Tom **nor** his brother. 我既沒有看見 Tom，也沒有看見他的弟弟。

　2. He didn't like her, **nor** did I. 他不喜歡她，我也不喜歡她。

　3. He wasn't nervous, **nor** was I. 他不緊張，我也不緊張。

注意：在例句 2、3 中，**nor** 置於第二個對等子句句首時，主詞與動詞要倒裝。其他的否定對等連接詞如 neither, not only ... but also 等亦如此。

⑷ **but**、**yet**、**still**

這三個對等連接詞都表示「**對比**」或「**相反**」的語意。

　1. She is poor, **but** (she is) happy. 她窮，但是她快樂

　2. I am very busy, **but** he is not. 我很忙，但是他不忙。

　3. He tried hard, **yet** he failed. 他努力過但失敗了。

　4. She is very honest, **still** they don't trust her. 她很誠實，但是他們還是不信任她。

⑸ **so** 與 **for**

so 表示結果；**for** 表示原因。例如：

　1. He was sick yesterday, **so** he was absent. 他昨天生病，所以缺席了。

2. She did not like him, *for* he was unreliable. 她不喜歡他,因爲他不可靠。

(6) *not only ... but* (*also*)

1. They *not only* came, *but* they *also* helped us clean the house. 他們不但來了, 還幫忙我們清掃房子。
2. *Not only* you *but* (*also*) he is tired. 不但你累了,他也累了。
3. *Not only did* she *babysit for us, but* she *also helped us with some housework*. 她不只替我們看小孩, 而且還幫忙做一點家事。

注意: 句子 not only 置子句首時, 主詞動詞的倒裝。

(7) *as well as*、*rather than* 等

1. She *as well as* you is tired.她和你都累了。
2. I want apples *rather than* oranges. 我想要蘋果, 而不是要橘子。
3. She *no less than* you is nervous. 她和你都緊張。

23.4. 從屬連接詞

23.4.1. 引導名詞子句的從屬連接詞

引導名詞子句的從屬連接詞常用的有: *that*、*what*、*when*、*who* (*m*)、*where*、*whose*、*which*、*how*、*why*、*if*、*whether* (*or not*)、*whatever*、 *whoever*、*whichever*、*whosever*、*because* 等。

　　名詞子句在句子中的功能與名詞相同，可以當主詞、受詞、補語等。以下分別舉例說明引導名詞子句的常用從屬連接詞。

⑴ *that*

1. I hope *that you will come here tomorrow*. 我希望你明天能來這兒。(做 hope 的受詞)

2. *That you did not come on time* is a pity. 你沒有準時來眞是可惜。(做 is 的主詞)

3. My answer is *that she is not able to help you*. 我的答案是，她沒法幫助你。(做主詞 answer 的補語)

4. We all know the fact *that she is honest*. 我們都知道的事實是，她是誠實的。(做名詞 fact 的同位語)。

有關 that 引導的名詞子句，下列還有兩點應注意。

⑷ that 子句作主詞時，除正式體裁以外，通常會使用引導詞 *it* 取代 that 子句的位置，而把 that 子句移至句末。例如：

1. *It* is a pity *that you did not come on time*. 很可惜你沒有準時來。

⒝引起名詞子句的 that，在非正式英語及口語中，常可省略。例如：

1. He said (*that*) *he would come on time*. 他說他會準時來。
2. It is a pity (*that*) *she can't help us.* 很可惜她不能幫我們。

⑵ *who*、*which*、*when*、*where*、*what*、*why*、*how*、*whether*(*or not*)、*if*

這些連接詞引導的名詞子句通常作動詞的受詞。例如：

1. Tell me *who she is*. 告訴我她是誰。(tell 的受詞)

2. We all know *when he will arrive*. 我們都知道他什麼時候到達。(know 的受詞)

3. I know *where he lives*. 我知道他住在哪裏。(know 的受詞)

4. I don't know *what she likes.* 我不知道她喜歡什麼。(know 的受詞)

5. Tell me *why you did it.* 告訴我你為何做這事。(tell 的受詞)

6. Tell me *how he did it.* 告訴我他是怎樣做這事的。(tell 的受詞)

7. No one knows *which he will choose*. 沒有人知道他會選哪一個。(know 的受詞)

8. I asked her *whether* (*or not*) *she would be nervous.* 我問她會不會緊張。(asked 的受詞)

9. I wonder *if*(或 *whether*) *she is interested in my plan.* 我不知道她是否對我的計劃感興趣。(wonder 的受詞)

(3) *whatever*、*whoever* 等

1. *Whoever comes late* will be punished. 無論誰遲到，就要受罰。(做 will be punished 的主詞)

2. You can do *whatever you like*. 你可以做任何你喜歡的事。(做 do 的受詞)

3. You may choose *whichever you like*. 你可以挑選你喜歡的任何一個。(做 choose 的受詞)

4. He can give the book to *whoever wants it*. 他可以把這本書給任何想要它的人。(做介詞 to 的受詞)

23.4.2.　引導形容詞子句的從屬連接詞

形容詞子句也就是關係子句。　因此引導形容詞子句的連接詞也就是關係代名詞及關係副詞：*who*、*whom*、*whose*、*that*、*when*、*where*、*why* 等。

形容詞子句的功能是修飾名詞，亦即其先行詞。以下是一些形容詞子句的例子。

1. He is a man *who(m) everyone respects.* 他是一個每個人都尊敬的人。

2. Where is the book *which/that he gave me*? 他給我的那本書在哪兒？

3. The book *whose cover is green* is mine. 綠色封面的那本書是我的。

4. Alice, *whose niece works for our company*, is a very good typist. Alice 是一位很好的打字員，她的姪女在我們的公司工作。

5. I know the time *when he will come*. 我知道他到達的時間。

有關形容詞子句(即關係子句)的更詳細用法及例句，請參看前面第二十二章。

23.4.3.　引導副詞子句的從屬連接詞

⑴時間副詞子句

引導時間副詞的從屬連接詞常用的有：*when*、*while*、*whenever*、*after*、*before*、*since*、*as*、*as soon as*、*once*、*till/until*、*as long as*、*next time*、*no sooner ... than* 等。

(A) *when*、*while*、*whenever*、*as*、*since*、*after*、*before* 等。例如：

1. I will do it *when I come back from Tainan*. 我從臺南回來就會做這事。

2. You can stay at our place *whenever you come to Taipei*. 無論什麼時候你到臺北來，都可住在我家。

3. Don't talk *while she is singing.* 她唱歌時不要講話。

4. *As he entered the room,* the phone rang. 當他進屋裏時，電話響了。

5. I have not seen him *since I came back from Hong Kong.* 我從香港回來以後就沒見過他。

6. I'll wait *until/till he comes.* 我會一直等到他來。

7. He came *after she had left.* 她走了之後他才來。

8. Please close the windows *before you leave this room.* 在你離開這房間之前，請把窗子關好。

(B) *as soon as*、 *no sooner ... than* 等。

表示「**立刻**」(一…就…)之意的副詞子句，最常用的連接詞為 *as soon as* 以及類似的連接詞如 *the minute*、*the moment* 等。例如：

1. He wrote to me $\left\{\begin{array}{l}\text{as soon as}\\\text{the moment}\\\text{the minute}\\\text{the instant}\end{array}\right\}$ he heard the news.

他一聽到這消息，就寫信給我。

此外，比較正式的用法有 *no sooner ... than* 等連接詞，例如：

2. He had $\left\{\begin{array}{l}\text{no sooner}\\\text{hardly}\\\text{scarcely}\end{array}\right\}$ entered the room $\left\{\begin{array}{l}\text{than}\\\text{when}\\\text{when}\end{array}\right\}$ the phone rang.

他一進房間，電話就響了。

例2的用法相當正式，並不常用。初學者應先學例1的用法。特別是 as soon as。

(C) *as long as*/*so long as*、*once*、*next time*、*every time*、*by the time* 等。

1. You can live here *as long as you pay the rent*. 只要你付房租，就可以住在這兒。

2. I will finish my report *by the time you return from your trip*. 到你旅行回來時，我將會做好我的報告。

3. *Once you enter the house*, you will be safe. 一旦你進入屋子裏，你就安全了。

4. He always gives me a call, *every time he comes to Taipei.* 每次他來臺北都會打電話給我。

5. Please give me a call *next time you come to Taipei.* 下一次你來台北時請給我打個電話。

(2)地方副詞子句

引導地方副詞子句的從屬連接詞有 *where*、*wherever*。例如：

1. You can stay *where you are.* 你可以逗留在你現在所在之處。

2. ***Wherever you go*** I will go . 你到哪裏，我就到那裏去。

3. Please put the key ***where you can find it again.*** 請把鑰匙放在你可以再找到它的地方。

⑶目的副詞子句

常用的連接詞有：***so that***、***in order that*** 等。例如：

$$I\ got\ up\ early \begin{Bmatrix} \textbf{\textit{so that}} \\ \textbf{\textit{in order that}} \end{Bmatrix} \textbf{\textit{I might catch the}}\ 6:00$$

train. 我一早起床是爲了要趕6點的火車。

⑷原因或理由副詞子句

常用的連接詞有：***because***、***since***、***as***、***now***、***that*** 等。例如：

1. I will help you ***because I like you.*** 因爲我喜歡你，我會幫助你。

2. ***Since she does not have enough money,*** she can't buy that dress. 因爲她的錢不夠，她不能買那件洋裝。

3. ***As he was on vacation,*** he did not know that his secretary had resigned. 因爲他正在渡假，他不知道他的秘書已經辭職了。

4. ***Now that you are here,*** please help me with this math problem. 既然你來了，就請幫忙我做這數學題目吧。

另外，在「be＋形容詞」後面，***that*** 也可以引導表示原因/理由的副詞子句。例如：

5. I am sorry ***that you don't like it.*** 你不喜歡它，我覺得很不安。

6. I am glad ***that you passed the exam.*** 我很高興你考試及格

了。

⑸條件副詞子句

常用的連接詞有：*if*、*in case*(*that*)、*unless*、*as long as*、*pro-vided*/*providing*(*that*)、*on condition* (*that*)、*suppose*/*supposing* (*that*)等。例如：

1. *If she likes it*, she will buy it. 如果她喜歡的話，她就會把它買下來。

2. *In case* (*that*) *she is not at home,* we will have to wait for her. 如果她不在家，我們就必須等她。

3. You don't have to be worried, *unless you did something wrong*. 除非你做錯了什麼事，你不必擔心。

4. You may use my kitchen *as long as you keep it clean*. 只要你保持清潔，你就可以使用我的廚房。

5. I will forgive you *on condition*/*provided that you do not do it again.* 如果你不再做這事，我就會原諒你。

6. *Suppose*/*Supposing* (*that*) *it rains tomorrow,* shall we stay at home? 假如明天下雨，我們要待在家嗎？

⑹結果副詞子句

常用的連接詞有：*so … that*、*such … that*。實際使用時，句式為：

> *so*＋形容詞/副詞…＋*that*…
> *such*＋名詞…＋*that*…

例如：

1. She was *so tired that she went to bed right after dinner*. 她那麼累，（以致於）一吃完晚飯就去睡。

2. She was *such a nice girl that everybody liked her*. 她是那麼好的一個女孩子，(以致於)每個人都喜歡她。

(7)比較副詞子句

比較副詞子句以連接詞 *than* 及 *as* 引導。例如：

1. The math problem is harder *than I thought*. 這數學題目比我想像中還要難。

2. He runs faster *than John* (*does*). 他跑的比 John 快。

3. I am not so clever *as you* (*are*). 我沒有你那麼聰明。

有關比較句式更多的例句，參看第十六、十七兩章。

(8)狀態副詞子句

常用的連接詞有：*as*、*as if*、*as though* 等。例如：

1. You may do *as I told you*. 你可以照我吩咐去做。

2. It ended *as I expected*. 這事正如我預期一樣地結束了。

3. She looks $\begin{Bmatrix} as\ if \\ as\ though \end{Bmatrix}$ *she is getting better.* 她看起來好像好了一些。

這句雖然用 as if 或 as though，但子句的內容接近事實(因為她的確是好了一些，或至少可能好了一些)。因此，子句中的動詞可以用現在式。

假如 as if 或 as though 句子引起的子句內容與事實相反時，就要用「假設時式」了。例如：

4. She treats me $\begin{Bmatrix} as\ if \\ as\ though \end{Bmatrix}$ *I were a stranger.* Actually, we have been good friends for years. 她把我當作陌生人看待。事實上，我們是多年的好朋友了。

句 4 之副詞子句中的 be 動詞要用假設時式 were，因爲子句的句意與事實不符。有關「假設句」的詳細情形，參看以下第二十四章。

(9)讓步/退讓副詞子句

讓步/退讓副詞子句表示「**雖然**」、「**即使**」等語意。常用的連接詞有：*though*、*although*、*even if*、*even though*、*while* 等。例如：

1. $\begin{Bmatrix} \textit{Though} \\ \textit{Although} \end{Bmatrix}$ he is poor, he is happy. 他雖然窮，但很快樂。

2. $\begin{Bmatrix} \textit{Even if} \\ \textit{Even though} \end{Bmatrix}$ you don't like him, you have to see him.
   即使你不喜歡他，你還是得見他。

3. *While he has many friends,* he often feels lonely. 雖然他有很多朋友，但他常常覺得孤單/寂寞。

其他表示讓步的連接詞還有 *whether* (*or not*)、*whatever* 等複合詞，以及 *no matter*＋疑問詞。例如：

4. *Whether he has enough money or not,* he is getting married. 不管他錢夠或不夠，他還是要結婚。

5. $\begin{Bmatrix} \textit{No matter what you say,} \\ \textit{Whatever you may say,} \end{Bmatrix}$ I won't listen to you. 不管你說什麼，我都不會聽你。

6. *Whoever they are* (*may be*), don't let them in. 無論他們是誰，都不要讓他們進來。

7. *However intelligent he is* (*may be*), I won't hire him.
   不管他多聰明，我都不會雇用他。

8. $\begin{Bmatrix} \textit{Wherever} \\ \textit{No matter where} \end{Bmatrix}$ you go, I'll miss you. 無論你到哪兒，

我都會想念你。

⑽對比副詞子句

引導對比副詞子句的從屬連接詞爲 *while* 及 *whereas*。例如：

1. Prof.Wang teaches phonetics, *while* Prof. Chang teaches syntax. 王敎授敎語音學，而張敎授則敎句法學。

2. I am learning English, *whereas* he is learning Spanish. 我正在學英文，而他正在學西班牙文。

23.5.　連副詞 therefore、however 等

英語中有些字像 *therefore*、*however*、*for example* 等，有些文法書視爲對等連接詞。但事實上這些字與對等連接詞不完全一樣。這些字可以置於子句前、中、後的三種位置，而對等連接詞則不可。例如：

She was sick; *therefore,* she was absent from class yesterday. 她生病了；所以昨天她缺席沒上課。

這句也可寫成：She was sick； she was, *therefore,* absent from class yesterday.或 She was sick; she was absent from class yesterday,*therefore*.(句末位置比較不常用)。

　　因此，有些文法書把這類字稱爲**連副詞**(conjunctive adverbs)，有別於一般的連接詞。事實上，這些連副詞的功能主要是句子之間語氣的承上轉下，所以也叫做「**語氣承轉詞**」(transitional devices)。對初階學生而言，這類連接用語最常用的有：*first* ‘第一’、*second* ‘第二’、*first of all* ‘首先’、*next* ‘其次’、*finally* ‘最後’、*in addition to* ‘除此之外’、*in the same way* ‘同樣地’、*therefore* ‘所以’、*so* ‘所以’、*for example* ‘比方

說'、*for instance* '比方說'、*in fact* '事實上'、*in other words* '換言之'、*especially* '特別地'、*at the same time* '同時'、*at once* '馬上'、*to sum up* '綜合而言'、*otherwise* '否則'、*however* '然而'、*after all* '畢竟'、*anyway* '無論如何'、*besides* '除此之外'　等。

　　這類詞語初學者只需略加認識即可。

23.6.　再說句子結構

　　先前我們對句子的分析，多只限於**簡單句** （simple sentence）。經過本章介紹連接詞以後，我們知道可以經由連接詞的連接，產生含兩個或兩個以上的子句的較長句子。因此，英文的句子可分以下四種：

⑴**簡單句**(simple sentence)含一個獨立子句。

　　例如：John is a student. John 是學生。

　　　　　He saw her yesterday. 他昨天見到她。

⑵**併合句**(compound sentence)，含兩個或多個對等子句。

　　例如：I like you but John likes her. 我喜歡你，但是 John 卻喜歡她。

⑶**複合句**(complex sentence)，含一個主要子句及一個或多個從屬子句。

　　例如：He said that he saw me. 他說他看見了我。

　　　　　He said that he saw me when he was eating his lunch. 他說當他在吃午飯時看見了我。

⑷**併複混合句**(compound-complex sentence)，同時含有複合句及併合句的句子。

　　例如：He said that he saw Tom when he was eating his

lunch but actually the person he saw was Peter. 他說當他吃中飯的時候他看見 Tom，但事實上他所看到的人是 Peter。

《習題 27》

(A)在以下各句中，將名詞子句用底線標示出來，並説明該子句在主要子句中的功能（如主詞、受詞等）。

例：I think *that he is honest*.
    受詞

1. I know how he becomes successful.

2. I don't know what I will do.

3. He wonders what she wants.

4. She told me that Tom wouldn't come.

5. Can you guess what I mean?

6. That he should say so is very natural.

7. I don't see how Ken can do it without my help.

8. Larry said that his mother was ill.

9. It all depends on how you do it.

10. I want you to pay attention to what I have to say.

11. My wish is that I may see you next fall.

12. There is no meaning in what she said.

13. The fact that she is a good student is well known to all.

14. This is what I want.

15. No one knows who he is.

(B)以名詞子句完成下列各句。

　例：I know _____ .

　　　I know *that he is honest.*

1. I think _____ .

2. They all said _____ .

3. I wonder _____ .

4. The report _____ is true.

5. It is certain _____ .

6. Have you heard _____ ?

7. This is _____ .

8. Do you know _____ .

9. _____ is natural.

10. Can you tell me _____ ?

11. Please pay attention to _____ .

12. Ken knows _____ .

13. His wish is _____ .

14. It is clear _____ .

15. She was pleased with _____ .

(C)用名詞子句來取代下面各句中斜體之部分。

　例：I don't know *the time of his coming.*

　　　I don't know when he will come.

1. No one knows *the time of his arrival.*

2. We heard *of his success.*

3. I know *him to be honest.*

4. We all hope *for his success.*

5. She knows *his birth place.*

(D)在以下各句中，以底線標出形容詞子句，並指出其修飾的名詞或代名詞。

例: This is the book *that he wrote*. (修飾 book)

1. This is the house that John built.

2. Students who are honest are trustworthy(可信賴的).

3. The plan you proposed is not practical.

4. He told us a story that is unbelievable.

5. Tom is the boy whose father is our teacher.

6. God helps those who help themselves.

7. Do you know anyone that doesn't like money?

8. He is the cleverest boy that I have ever seen.

(E)以形容詞子句完成下列各句。

例: I know the boy _____ .

I know the boy *who is standing over there*.

1. I know the place _____ .

2. Morton is a man _____ .

3. The house _____ is a very old one.

4. The boy _____ won the prize.

5. I found my pen _____ .

6. Any student _____ will be punished.

7. You are looking at the girl _____ .

8. She is the only woman _____ .

(F)在以下各句中，以底線標出副詞子句，並註明是何種副詞子句。

例: They rested *when evening came*.

(時間副詞子句)

1. You may go wherever you want to.

2. I have not seen him after I came back.

3. She will do it when she is ready.

4. She wrote to me as soon as she got there.

5. Once you enter the room, you will be safe.

6. You will pass the exam if you work hard.

7. We will wait until you come.

8. He turned on the light because the room was dark.

9. As he was not at home, I told his son that I would call again.

10. I am sorry that you don't like it.

11. He does not always speak as he thinks.

12. If you don't come on time, we will go ahead without you.

13. He was so busy that he did not have the time to do his homework.

14. She runs as fast as Jane.

15. Although he worked hard, he did not pass the exam.

(G)以適當的副詞子句完成下列各句。

　　例：I was eating lunch ＿＿＿＿＿＿＿．

　　　　I was eating lunch *when he came in.*

1. I was so busy ＿＿＿＿＿＿＿．

2. She ran so fast ＿＿＿＿＿＿＿．

3. Don't say anything to him ＿＿＿＿＿＿＿．

4. He spoke in such a low voice ＿＿＿＿＿＿＿．

5. I won't do it ＿＿＿＿＿＿＿．

6. ＿＿＿＿＿＿＿, you will become ill.

7. ＿＿＿＿＿＿＿, I won't listen to you.

8. I will punish you ＿＿＿＿＿＿＿．

9. We were happy _____.

10. He wrote to me _____.

11. You may come to see me _____.

12. _____, I am happy.

13. I did not pay the bill _____.

14. She felt confused _____.

15. I ran away _____.

(H)指出下列各句的類別。

例： a. I am a student but he is a teacher.（併合句）

b. I know that he is a student.（複合句）

c. He said that I was wrong but she thought that I was right.

（併複混合句）

d. He came in order to see me.（簡單句）

1. I went to the party because I was invited.

2. Run faster, or they will overtake（趕過）you.

3. Either he is too nervous or she is too excited.

4. He was standing there smoking a cigarette.

5. They asked him how he got there, but he refuse to answer.

6. This is the book that you want me to buy.

7. I said nothing to them.

8. He came early but she was late.

第二十四章
條件句與假設句

24.1. 假設時式

英語中有些句子需要使用與一般時式不一樣的「**假設時式**」(hypothetical tenses)。使用假設時式的句子是一些表達假設語意的句子。這些假設句子包括幾種 *if* 引導的條件句以及含有動詞 *wish*、*suggest* 和由 *as if*、*as though* 引導的假設句子。

假設時式有三種:

(1)「**原式**」,如 *be*、*go* 等。用於 *insist*、*suggest* 等後面。

(2)「**簡單過去式**」,如 *were*、*went*、*did* 等。表示與現在或將來有關的假設。

(3)「**過去完成式**」,如 *had been*、*had done* 等。表示與過去有關的假設。

24.2. 條件句

24.2.1. 第 1 類條件句

第 1 類條件句中 if 子句的語意是中立的, 亦即是這些條件可能實現, 也可能不實現。其時式用法如下:

If 子句	主要子句
現在式	現在式/將來式(*will*、*can*、*may* 等＋V)

例如:

1. If she *takes* a taxi, she *will get* there in time. 如果她坐計程車, 她就會及時趕到那兒。
2. If you *touch* me again, *I'll scream*. 如果你再碰我, 我就會大叫。
3. If you *finish* your work, you *can go* home. 如果你做完你的工作, 就可以回家。

24.2.2. 第 2 類條件句

⑴時式

If 子句	主要子句
過去式	*would*＋V 或 *could*、*might* 等＋V

⑵這類條件句指的是現在或將來, 主要表示兩種語意:

(A)與現在事實相反(或不可能)的假設。例如:

1. I don't have enough money right now. If I *had* enough money, I *would buy* a car. 我現在沒有足夠的錢。如果我有足夠的錢，我就會買一部汽車。(現在與事實相反)

2. If I *were* you, I *would listen* to him. 如果我是你的話，我就會聽他的。(現在不可能)

(B)說話者預期這種動作不會發生。例如:

1. If Tom *worked* harder next time, he *would pass* the exam. 如果下一次更用功一點，Tom 考試就會及格了。(將來; 但說話者預期 Tom 不會更用功)

24.2.3.　第 3 類條件句

(1)時式

If　子句	主要子句
過去完成式	*would*＋*have*＋過 去 分 詞(或 *would*、*should*、*might* 等＋過去分詞)

(2)這類條件句指的是過去。表示主要子句的動作沒有實現或做成，因為 if 子句中的動作沒有發生或沒有做。這是所謂「**與過去事實相反的假設**」。例如:

1. If he *had helped* her, she *would have been* grateful to him. 如果(當時)他幫助過她，她會感激他。(事實上他沒有幫過她，而她也並不感激他。)

2. If they *had asked* me, I *might have given* them some

hints. 如果(當時)他們問過我，我可能會給他們一些提示。(事實上那時候他們沒問我，我也沒給他們提示。)

24.2.4. could／would／should／might 等＋ have＋過去分詞

　　could／would／should／might 等＋have＋過去分詞用於第 3 類條件句的主要子句時，表示過去沒有實現的動作。事實上，即使不是用於條件句中，這些動詞形式都具有這種含意。例如：

1. She asked me for my help but I turned her down. I ***should have helped her***. 她請求我幫她忙但我拒絕了。我本該幫她忙的。

2. Nancy was very lucky. She ***might have been killed*** in the accident. Nancy 很幸運，她本來可能在這意外事件中喪生的。(但是她並沒有死)

24.3. 假設句

　　除了 if 子句可以表示假設說法以外，還有好些句式可以表示假設。我們把 if 子句以外而能表示假設意思的句子通稱為假設句。

24.3.1. 某些定型的套語

　　這些定型的用語或說法常常表示祈許、願望。時式用「原式」。例如：

1. God *bless* you! 天主/上帝保祐你!

2. God *save* the queen! 天祐女皇!

3. *Come* what may, I will go ahead with my plan. 不管發生什麼事情, 我都會照計畫行事。

24.3.2. as if 與 as though

as if/*as though* 後面如果假設情況時, 通常要用假設時式。而句子通常蘊含「否定的推測/推斷」。例如:

1. She *acts as if*/*as though* she *knew* you. 她表現得好像認識你的樣子。(暗示: 她不認識你)

2. The boy acted *as if*/*as though* he had *done* something wrong. 那個男孩(當時)表現得好像做錯了什麼事的樣子。(暗示: 他並沒有做錯事)

24.3.3. order、insist、suggestion、important 等

英語有些名詞、動詞、或形容詞後面接 that 子句, 表示某種「強制」的語意(如 '必須'、'堅持'、'命令' 等)。這些 that 子句中通常用假設時式中的「原式」。

⑴這類動詞常用者有: *ask* '要求'、*demand* '要求'、*insist* '堅持'、*order* '命令'、*propose* '建議'、*prefer* '寧願要, 比較喜歡'、*request* '請求'、*suggest* '建議、提議'等。例如:

1. The manager *insists* that Peter *resign*. 經理堅持要 Peter 辭職。

2. I *suggest* that we *reconsider* her application. 我提議我們重新考慮她的申請。

(2)這類形容詞常用者有：*advisable* '明智的'、*essential* '必須的、重要的'、*important* '重要的'、*necessary* '必須的'、*urgent* '緊急的'等。例如：

1. It is *essential* that he *reconsider* his resignation.　他重新考慮他的辭呈是必須的。

2. It is *important* that he *make* no comment on this.　很重要的是，他對此事不發表評論。

(3)這類名詞常用的有：*decision* '決定'、*demand* '要求'、*order* '命令'、*insistence* '堅持'、*requirement* '要求'、*proposal* '建議'、*suggestion* '提議'等。例如：

1. We all like the *proposal* that tax *be* abolished. 我們都喜歡廢除賦稅的建議。

2. We can't understand the manager's *insistence* that Peter *resign* immediately. 對於經理堅持 Peter 馬上辭職，我們都無法了解。

注意：以上三種「強制」語意的句形中，that 子句動詞除用「原式」外，也可用「*should*＋原式」。

例如：I suggest that we *should reconsider* his application.　大致上，美式英語比較喜歡用「原式」。

24.3.4.　wish

　　主要子句的動詞如為 **wish**，可接 **that** 子句作受詞，如果 that 子句的語意為假設語意，就要用假設時式。例如：

1. I **wish** (**that**) she **were** here. 但願她在這兒。（與現在事實相反；她現在不在這兒。）
2. They **wish** (**that**) they **had joined** the club. 他們希望參加了這個俱樂部。（但事實上，他們‘當時’沒有參加；與過去事實相反。）
3. I told him that I **wished** I **had invited** her to the party. 我告訴他說我真希望我邀請了她參加聚會。（但事實上‘當時’我沒有邀請過她；與過去事實相反。）

《習題 28》

(A)填入適當的動詞形式。

1. If I find your pen, I _____ (give) you a call.
2. You can use my telephone, if yours _____ (not work).
3. If the elevator(電梯) does not work, we _____ (have) to use the stairs.
4. If you _____ (finish) your homework, you can go out and play.
5. If it _____ (rain) tomorrow, we will not go to the park.
6. If I had a million dollars, I _____ (buy) her a diamond ring.
7. If he gave me the job, I _____ (take) it.

8. I would be very happy if I _____ (be) you.

9. If she sold her car, she _____ (get) only one thousand dollars.

10. Tom was only nineteen. If he _____ (be) twenty-one, he would be able to use the money from that fund(基金).

11. I would have sent you a letter if I _____ (have) your address.

12. If they _____ (asked) him twice, he would have accepted the job.

13. If he had driven faster, we _____ (get) there in time.

14. If there had been a phone, I _____ (call) you.

15. If I had waited a little longer, I _____ (see) her.

(B)填入適當的動詞形式。

1. I am not rich. I wish I _____ (be) rich.

2. I am not tall. I would like to be taller. I wish I _____ (be) taller.

3. I can't afford a new apartment. I wish I _____ (can afford) a new apartment.

4. It's hot. I wish it _____ (be) cool.

5. I live in Taipei. I wish I _____ (live) in Taichung.

(C)完成下列各句。

例：If it rains tomorrow ...

    If it rains tomorrow, *we will stay home.*

1. If I were you,...

2. If you help me,...

3. If he had enough time,...

4. I wish I ...

5. If she had come earlier,...

6. If we had finished our homework,...

7. If you come on time ...

8. It is important that,...

9. The captain insisted that ...

10. I don't like his suggestion that ...

第二十五章
引導詞 It 與 There

25.1. 引導詞 It 與 There

英語的 *it* 與 *there* 都有些特殊的用法。可以在句子中取代主詞或受詞的位置，本身却是不具語意的虛詞。例如：

1. *It* is important to be on time. 準時是重要的一回事。

2. *There* are two books on the desk. 桌上有兩本書。

例句 1 與 2 的眞正主詞分別是不定詞片語 to be on time 以及名詞組 two books。It 與 There 雖然在主詞的位置上，但是却是沒有語意的「**虛詞**」。文法書中稱爲「**前設主詞**」(preparatory subject) 或「**臨時主詞**」(temporary subject)。我們可以把句 1 與 2 的眞正主詞放回主詞的位置，就不難明白 it 與 there 的「**虛詞**」性質了。

1.a. *To be on time* is important.

2.a. *Two books* are on the desk.

句 1 a 與 2 a 的意思與句 1、2 相同。由此可見 it 與 there 只是代替或「引導」眞正的主詞。這兩字的用法有好幾種。以下我們均以「**引導詞** *it*」與「**引導詞** *there*」來通稱之。

25.2. 引導詞 It

25.2.1.

引導詞 *it* 作「前設主詞」常用於以下的結構:

$$\left\{ \begin{array}{l} \textit{That 子句} \\ \text{不定詞片語} \end{array} \right\} + \textit{be} + \left\{ \begin{array}{l} \text{NP} \\ \text{Adj} \end{array} \right\} \longrightarrow$$

$$\textit{It} + \textit{be} + \left\{ \begin{array}{l} \text{NP} \\ \text{Adj} \end{array} \right\} + \left\{ \begin{array}{l} \textit{that 子句} \\ \text{不定詞片語} \end{array} \right\}$$

例如:

1. *To be on time* is important. 準時是重要的。

   It is important *to be on time*.

2. *For you to be there on time* is important. 你準時到那兒是重要的一回事。

   It is important *for you to be there on time*.

3. *That he is very lazy* is true. 他很懶,這是眞的。

   It is true *that he is very lazy*.

以上 3 例句, 雖然都有兩種說法, 但是在日常使用時, 除正式文體以外, 都是以引導詞 *It* 開首的說法比較自然。其他一些例子如下:

4. *It* is nice *to be here*. 來到這兒眞好。

5. It is surprising *that he should like English*. 他居然喜歡英文, 眞是令人驚訝。

6. *It* is not easy *to find a good job*. 找一份好工作並不容易。

7. *It* is a pity *to miss the train*. 錯過了這班火車是可惜的事。

8. *It* is a pity *that you didn't pass the exam*. 你沒有通過考試眞是可惜。

注意：

(a)有一些 V-ing 的結構，也可以用 it 作「**前設主詞**」。例如：

9. It was nice *seeing you at Tom's party*. 在 Tom 的聚會中看到你眞好。

10. It is worth *helping him*. 幫助他是値得的。

(b)大多數的不定詞結構如帶有「**主詞**」時，介詞會用 *for*。例如 for you to come here, for him to say something 等。但如句子本身主詞的形容詞如表示某人對某事的態度時，介詞常會用 *of*。例如：

11. It is *kind of* him to help me. 他幫我，眞是好心。

25.2.2.

前設主詞 *it* 後面也可接連繫動詞 *seem*、*appear*。例如：

1. It *seems* that Alice has been working very hard. Alice 似乎一直都很用功。

2. It *appears* that she is very confused. 看起來她很困惑。

3. It *seems* possible that she will find a good job. 看起來她可能會找到一份好工作。

25.2.3.

除 that 子句以外，wh 字所引導的名詞子句也可用於這種句式。例如：

1. *It* was amazing *how he can learn to speak English so well*. 他能學會說那麼好的英語，眞令人驚異。

2. *It* doesn't matter *when you come*. We will be waiting for you at home. 你什麼時候來都沒關係。我們會在家裏等你。

3. *It* is doubtful *whether* (*or not*) *he will come on time*. 他會不會準時來，還是疑問。

4. *It* is a mystery *why Larry left home*. Larry 爲了什麼離家是一個謎。

5. *It* is not clear *what Tom wants*. Tom 想要什麼並不很清楚。

6. *It* does not matter *where we'll stay*. 我們要待在哪兒都沒關係。

25.2.4.

英語有一種句式叫做「**分裂句**」，專門用來強調句子中的某一詞組。被強調的詞組置於引導詞 it 後面。其形式如下：

$$It + be + \text{被強調的詞組} + \begin{Bmatrix} that(\text{事、物、人}) \\ who(\text{人}) \end{Bmatrix} \cdots$$

例如：

1. *John* went *there yesterday*. John 昨天去過那兒。

句1的 *John*、*there* 及 *yesterday* 都可用上面分裂句式分別加以強調。

2. *It* was *John that* (*who*) went there yesterday. 昨天去過那兒的人是 *John*。

3. *It* was *there that* John went yesterday. John 昨天去的地方是**那兒**。

4. **It** was **yesterday that** John went there. John 是**昨天去那兒**的。

25.2.5.

引導詞 **it** 也可以作「**前設受詞**」(anticipatory object)。例如:

1. I find **it** hard **to do this work alone**. 我覺得獨力做這工作很不容易。

例句1的 **it** 是虛詞, 真正的受詞是 to do … alone。其他的例子如:

2. We considered **it** a pity **that he left early**. 我們認為他提早離開是一件可惜的事。

3. She thinks **it** wrong **to tell lies**. 她認為撒謊是不對的。

4. I make **it** a rule **to go to bed early**. 我維持早睡的習慣。

5. I made **it clear that no one should leave early**. 我很清楚的表示過, 沒有人可以早走。

25.3. 引導詞 There

There 有兩種唸法, 語意和詞類也不同。當副詞使用時唸重音 [ðɛr], 意思是「**那裏**」; 當引導詞(前設主詞)使用時, 唸 [ðɚ](不唸重音), 是不具語意的虛詞。例如:

1. He is over **there** [ðɛr]. 他在那邊。

2. **There** [ðɚ] is a book on the desk. 桌上有一本書。

例句2之 there 是虛詞; there 當引導主詞時, 動詞與後面的真正主詞一致, 如例句2用 is, 但以下例句3、4就得用 are:

3. There *are three books* on the desk. 桌上有三本書。

4. There *are a pen and a book* on the desk. 桌上有一枝筆和一本書。

注意：例句 4 在非正式的口語中，也可以說成 There *is* a pen and a book on the desk.

25.3.1.　There＋be

有三種常用句式：

(1) *There＋be＋* $\left\{ \begin{array}{l} \text{名詞} \\ \text{代名詞} \end{array} \right\}$ ＋表示處所用語

1. There is a boy *here*. 這兒有個男孩子。

2. The is a pen *in my drawer*. 我的抽屜裏面有一枝筆。

3. There are no students *in the classroon*. 教室裏面沒有學生。

(2) *There＋be＋*帶修飾語的名詞組

1. There are *some* people *who can help you*. 有一些人可以幫助你。

2. There is a student *who wants to study psychology*. 有一個學生想唸心理學。

3. There are *two* pencils *for everyone*. 每人有兩枝鉛筆。

(3) *There＋be＋*名詞＋分詞修飾語

1. There is someone *waiting for you at the door*. 有人在門口等你。

2. There is a sale *going on at Fedco*. Fedco 公司正在減價中。

3. There were three students *injured in the accident*. 有三個學生在意外事件中受傷。

25.3.2.　There＋seem、appear 等

除 be 動詞以外，其他連繫動詞如 *seem*、*appear*、*remain* 以及動詞 *come*、*go*、*enter*、*follow*、*live*、*happen* 等都可以與引導詞 *there* 連用（在文學作品及正式文體中尤其如此）。例如：

1. *There* once *lived* a witch. 從前有一個女巫。

2. *There remained* two problems. 還有兩個問題。

3. *There seems* to be no good excuse for his failure. 他的失敗似乎沒有好的藉口。

4. *There goes* Peter. Peter 走了。

5. *There entered* the big bad wolf. 大惡狼進來了。

《習題 29》

(A)做照例句，做句式轉換。

例： a. That he is happy is obvious.

　　　It is obvious that he is happy.

　　b. To be on time is important.

　　　It is important to be on time.

　　c. For him to be on time is important.

　　　It is important for him to be on time.

1. That he has lost his courage(勇氣) is obvious.

2. That Larry failed in the exam is a pity.

3. That Mary can do the job alone is possible.

4. That Tom had stolen the money was true.

5. Whether he will come or not is not certain.

6. For me to find a good job is not difficult.

7. That no one here likes Betty is a fact.

8. You are kind to let me use your phone.

9. To speak loudly in public is impolite.

10. For him to come up with(想出) a good idea is not easy.

11. To see you here is nice.

12. To be honest is important.

(B)以下各句中，a 部分描述一件事情的性質(如 Something is easy.)，b 部分寫出這件事情本身(如 She is happy.)。請(1)以 for ... to V 方式改寫 b 部分，再與 a 部分合成一句；(2)把合併之句子改以引導詞 it 的句式重寫。

例：
a. Something is easy.
b. She is happy. } →

　(1) *For* her *to* be happy is easy.

　(2) *It* is easy for her to be happy.

1. a. Something is possible.
   b. He earns a million dollars. } →

2. a. Something would be a pity.
   b. You miss the English class. } →

3. a. Something will be a mistake.
   b. I go to Tom's party. } →

4. a. Something is dangerous.
   b. They play basketball in the street. } →

5. a. Something is strange.
   b. He writes poems(詩). } →

6. a. Something is difficult.
   b. I learn to speak French. } →

7. a. Something is a good idea.
   b. We play hide-and-seek(捉迷藏). } →

8. a. Something is nice.
   b. We take a short break. } →

(C)按照(B)的方式，以 that 子句改寫下面各句。

例：　a. Something is true.
　　　b. She is happy. } →

　　　(1) *That* she is happy is true.

　　　(2) *It* is true *that* she is happy.

1. a. Something is interesting.
   b. He can speak five languages. } →

2. a. Something is amazing.
   b. She won the first price in the contest. } →

3. a. Something is a fact.
   b. She is a naughty girl. } →

4. a. Something is a shame.
   b. Larry cheated in the exam. } →

5. a. Something is a fact.
   b. She is the only heir to that fontune. } →

6. a. Something is certain.
　 b. He is a brave soldier. } →

7. a. Something seems possible.
　 b. He will be admitted to a national university. } →

8. a. Something seems obvious.
　 b. She is a good teacher. } →

⒟ 以分裂句式(It ... that ...)來強調下列句子中畫底線的部分。

例： John gave me *a book*.

　　 It was *a book that* John gave me.

1. I saw Claudia *yesterday*.

2. *I* do not want to come.

3. Larry found *a doll* under the desk.

4. Larry found a doll *under the desk*.

5. *Larry* found a doll under the desk.

6. *John* is the first one to arrive.

7. Steve tried to save *the child*.

8. He puts *the book* on the desk.

9. *He* puts the book on the desk.

10. He puts the book *on the desk*.

⒠ 填入適當的 be 動詞。除特別註明者以外，一律用現在式。

1. There ＿＿＿＿＿＿a blackboard in the classroom.

2. There ＿＿＿＿＿＿three boys at the party. (過去式)

3. There ＿＿＿＿＿＿some mistakes in your homework.

4. There ＿＿＿＿＿＿about 500 guests at Tom's party. (過去式)

5. There ＿＿＿＿＿＿only one student who is willing to help us.

6. There _____ two pencils in my drawer.
7. There _____ a little milk in the bottle.

第二十六章
基本溝通功能的表達

26.1. 溝通功能與文法結構

我們都知道, 使用語言的目的主要在**溝通**(communicate)。基本的**溝通功能**(communicate functions)有: 陳述、詢問、引述、否定、命令(祈使)、強調、請求、勸告、建議、感嘆等。

我們平日說話或寫作,大多以達成上述這些功能為主要目的。在英語中, 我們也有各種文法結構, 表示上述的基本溝通功能, 例如陳述句、否定句、命令(祈使)句、問句等等。在這一章中, 我們將分別討論表達基本溝通功能的各種句式。

26.2. 陳述句、問句、否定句

⑴「**陳述**」事情的句子是「**陳述句**」(statements, 又叫做「**直述句**」)。例如:

1. Tom is a college student. Tom 是大學生。

2. They came here yesterday. 他們昨天到這兒來。

陳述句是我們日常最常用的句式之一。本章的例句絕對是陳述句。

(2)表示「**詢問**」的句子為「**問句**」(guestions)。例如：

1. Is she tired? 她累了嗎？

2. Will you come tomorrow? 你明天會來嗎？

3. What can we do? 我們能做什麼呢？

關於「**問句**」的詳細情形，參看本書第十章。

(3)表示「**否定**」的句子為「**否定句**」(negative sentences)。例如：

1. She is not my student. 她不是我的學生。

2. I will not do it. 我不會做這事。

3. He doesn't know my name. 他不知道我的名字。

4. She never comes here on Sunday. 星期天她從來都不會到這兒來。

關於「**否定句**」的詳細情形，參看本書第十一章。

26.3. 命令/祈使句

表示「**命令**」的常用句式是「**命令句**」(commands)或稱「**祈使句**」(imperatives)。其主要形式如下：

(1)主詞為第二人稱(因為命令句是直接對聽話者說的)。動詞用原式，否定詞用「***Don't***＋**動詞原式**」。主詞 you 通常不必說出來。例如：

1. ***Come*** in. (＝You come in.) 進來。

2. *Stop*! (＝You stop!) 停下來!

3. *Be* careful. (＝You must be careful.) 小心點。

4. *Don't stop*! (＝You don't stop!) 別停下來。

注意: ⒜ you 通常不用, 因為 You stop! you come here. 等說法比
　　　較不禮貌。

　　　⒝對話者的名字也可說出來。例如 Come here, Tom. 'Tom,你
　　　到這兒來。'

⑵主詞為第一及第三人稱時, 祈使句的形式為:

Let ⎰ *me* / *us* / *him* / *her* / *them* / *the boy* / 等 ⎱ ＋動詞原式

例如: 1. *Let me go*. 讓我走。

　　　2. *Let us help* you. 讓我們幫你吧。

　　　3. *Let those people come* in. 讓那些人進來吧。

　　　4. *Let them go* by bus. 讓他們坐公車去吧。

否定式為:

Don't ＋*let*＋ ⎰ *me* / *us* / *the boy* / 等 ⎱ ＋動詞原式

或

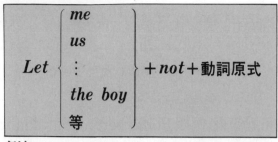

$$Let \left\{\begin{array}{l} me \\ us \\ \vdots \\ the\ boy \\ 等 \end{array}\right\} + not + 動詞原式$$

例如:

5. *Don't let them go.* 不要讓他們去。

6. *Let us not go* by bus. 讓我們不要坐公車去。

注意: *Let us* 可以說成 *Let's*。如 *Let's go.*

(3)在祈使句前加 Do, 可加強語氣。例如:

1. *Do be* careful! (千萬要/眞的要)小心點。

2. *Do hurry*! (千萬要/眞的要)趕快。

26.4. 強調句

「強調句」(emphatic sentences)主要有兩種方式:

(1)句子含有 be 動詞或助動詞時(包括主要助動詞及情態助動詞), 把句重音唸在 be 動詞助動詞上, 可強調整句句意。例如:

1. She *ís* here. 她是在這裏。

2. They *áre right.* 他們是對的。

3. I *háve* done my homework. 我已經做完功課了。

4. He *wíll* come tomorrow. 他明天會來的。

5. He *cán* do it. 這件事他做得到的。

⑵句子動詞爲不含助動詞的普通動詞時，在動詞前面加上適當形式的 **do** 動詞。重音唸在 **do** 上面，以強調句意。例如：

1. I **dó** believe that man. 我眞的相信那個人。

2. They **díd** give me that book. 他們眞的把那本書給了我。

3. Tom **dóes** have three sisters and four brothers. Tom 眞的有三個姊妹和四個兄弟。

26.5.　請求句

常用的「**請求句**」(requests)的句式如下：

$$
(1)\quad
\begin{Bmatrix}
\textit{Can} \\
\textit{Could} \\
\textit{May} \\
\textit{Might}
\end{Bmatrix}
+
\begin{Bmatrix}
\textit{I} \\
\textit{we}
\end{Bmatrix}
+ \text{V} \dots ?
$$

例如：

1. **Can** I have a cup of tea? 我可以要杯茶嗎？

2. **Could** you open the window? 你可以打開窗子嗎？

3. **May** I come in? 我可以進來嗎？

4. **Might** I speak to him? 我可以跟他說話嗎？

以上四種說法 can 最不正式，could 最普遍，may 與 might 最正式。這些句子，形式雖是問句，但說話者眞正的用意並不在於聽者的口頭回答，而在於請求被允許去做句子的動作。

$$(2) \begin{Bmatrix} Could \\ Would \\ Will \\ 等 \end{Bmatrix} + you + V \ldots ?$$

例如:

　　1. *Could* you（please）close the door? 請你關起門來，可以嗎?

　　2. *Would* you pass me the salt,（please）? 可以請你把鹽拿過來好嗎?

　　3. *Will* you（please）sit down? 請你坐下來，好嗎?

could you 與 would you 意思差不多，但 will you 的語氣比較不禮貌。

　　上面這三句雖然形式上是問句，但說話者真正的用意是請求聽者去做動詞所表達的動作，是常用的請求句。

　　其他常用的請求句形式有: *Would you mind* + V-*ing* …? *Would you like to* …? 等。例如:

　　4. *Would you mind coming in*? 請你進來好嗎?

　　5. *Would you like to have* a cup of tea? 請您喝杯茶好嗎?

26.6. 勸告句

「勸告句」（sentences expressing advice）中，常用的表示勸告的用語有: *must*、*should*、*ought to*、*had better*、*If I were you*、*I would* 或 *should* 等。例如:

　　1. You *must* try this soup.　It tastes marvellous. 你得嚐嚐這種湯。味道好極了。

2. You *had better* turn off the lights. 你最好還是把燈關掉。

3. *If I were you,* I *would* come tomorrow. 如果我是你的話，我就明天來。

26.7. 建議句

在「建議句」(sentences expressing suggestions)中，常用的表示建議的用語有：*let's*、*shall we*、*why don't you/we …?*、*why not*＋原式動詞、*what/how about*＋V-*ing/noun*、*suggest* 等。例如：

1. *Let's* go home now. 我們現在回家去吧!

2. *Shall* we invite all our friends? 我們邀請所有的朋友吧。

Let's 句後可接 *shall we*?作附加短問句。其語意功能也是提建議。例如：

3. *Let's* go home now, *shall we*? 我們現在回家去，好嗎?

Let's not＋原式可引導否定的建議。例如：

4. *Let's not do* it ourselves. (讓)我們不要自己動手做。

其他建議句的例子如：

5. *Why don't you* use my phone? 你何不就用我的電話呢?

6. *Why not say* hello to him?　為何不跟他打個招呼?

7. *What about eating* out tonight? 今天晚上到外面去吃飯如何?

8. *How about a hamberger*? 來一客漢堡如何?

9. {
  a. I *suggest* his buying the house.
  b. I *suggest* that he buy the house.
  c. I *suggest* that he should buy the house. 我建議他買那幢房子。

26.8.　感嘆句

表示驚嘆、痛苦、願望、高興等感情的句子稱為「**感嘆句**」(exclamatory sentences)，其後多加感嘆號(!)，感嘆句形式通常有兩種：

(1) *What* ＋(形容詞)＋名詞＋主詞＋動詞!

　1. *What a good student* he is! 他真是個好學生啊！（相對的陳述句是：He is a good student.）

　2. *What a beautiful day* it is! 今天天氣可真好啊！（相對的陳述句是：It is a beautiful day.）

(2) *How* ＋形容詞/副詞＋主詞＋動詞!

　1. *How clever she is!* 她好聰明啊！（相對的陳述句：She is clever.）

　2. *How efficiently he did* the job! 這件事他做得多麼有效率啊！（相對的陳述句：He did the job efficiently.）

《習題 30》

(A)將以下各句改為問句。

1. Mary can ski.

2. John saw Tom yesterday.

3. She is very intelligent.

4. He left very early this morning.

5. They turned off the lights.

6. Noel parked her car in front of the house.

7. He feels satisfied.

8. We took the exam yesterday.

9. He has just come back from the meeting.

10. I showed him his new office.

(B)將下列各句改為否定句。

1. I felt tired.

2. Jack was nervous.

3. He has been successful in business.

4. She has gone to bed.

5. They got off the bus.

6. Tom has two sisters.

7. I was standing around the corner.

8. She wants to put her dolls in a big box.

9. He did his best.

10. They want their children to stay home.

(C)將下列各句改為強調句。

例：He likes apples. → He *does* like apples.

1. We love our country.

2. I want to go to bed early tonight.

3. Tony needs a walkman.

4. He resembles his mother.

5. I want to paint the room pink.

6. I paid the bill.

7. He bought a new bicycle.

8. She usually drives carefully.

9. He took off his glasses.

10. I have a few questions to ask.

(D)將以下各句改為肯定及否定祈使句。

例：You come in.

肯定：*Come in.*

否定：*Don't come in.*

1. You stand up.

2. You sit down.

3. You must be careful.

4. You look at me.

5. You listen to what your mother has to say.

6. You go out.

7. You put the book on the shelf.

8. You take the letter to Tom.

9. You close the door.

10. You open the window.

(E)將下列各句改爲肯定及否定的祈使句。

例： He comes in.

　　肯定： *Let him come in.*

　　否定： *Don't let him come in.*

1. I go.

2. We help you.

3. They stay as long as they like.

4. She has fun.

5. I show you how to use it.

6. He eats his lunch.

7. She is your secretary.

8. She has a diamond ring.

(F)按以下提示之意，造適當的請求句。

例！ (I want to come in.)

　　May I come in?

　　或 *Could I come in?*

　　或 *Can I come in?*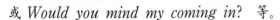

　　或 *Would you mind my coming in?*　等。

1. (I want to go out.)

2. (We want to sit here.)

3. (I want to talk to her.)

4. (I want you to open the door.)

5. (I want you to pass me the salt.)

6. (I want to stay here.)

7. (I want you to go upstairs.)

8. (We want to come tomorrow.)

(G)參考 12.6.及 12.7.之例句，造五句「勸告句」以及五句「建議句」。

(H)將下列各句改爲感嘆句。

　　例：He is a clever boy.→ *What a clever boy he is*!

　　　　He is clever.→ *How clever he is*!

1. Sandy is a beautiful girl.
2. It is a beautiful rose.
3. The rose smells sweet.
4. He looks tired.
5. He was lucky.
6. It is a beautiful day.
7. She runs fast.
8. They fought courageously(勇敢地).

第二十七章
直接引述與間接引述

27.1. 直接引述與間接引述

　　敍述某人所說過的話有兩種方式。其中一種是把原話一字不變地「**直接引述**」(direct speech)；另一種方式爲依照說話者原意重述，但原句的用詞並非完全重複，稱爲「**間接引述**」(indirect speech)。例如：

1. He said, "I have done my homework." 他說：「我已經做好功課了。」（直接引述原句；一字不改放在引號中。）
2. He said (that) he had done his homework. 他說他已經做好功課了。（間接引述）

　　「**直接引述**」不牽涉用詞的變化，因此，以下 27.2.節中只介紹其書寫形式。

　　「**間接引述**」因涉及一些動詞及代名詞指稱等變化，因此分別在 27.3.至 27.6.幾節中，分別討論間接引述陳述句、問句、命令句、請求句、建議句等的方式。

27.2. 直接引述

引述一個子句(陳述句、問句、或感嘆句)時，寫法有三種:

⑴如果**引述動詞**(如 say、ask 等)在句子前面時，在引述動詞後用**逗點**(comma)，引號後面引述原句的第一個單字要大寫，而原句之**句點**(period)則置於引號之內。例如:

1. She said, "My father is a lawyer." 她說:「我的父親是律師。」

2. He asked, "What will I do?" 他問說:「我要做什麼?」

3. He said, "What a pretty girl she is!" 他說:「她是多麼美麗的女孩子啊!」

⑵如果引述動詞在句末時,引述原句句末用逗點; 如引述問句或感嘆句時, 引述句仍用問號或感嘆號。例如:

1. "My father is a lawyer," she said. 「我父親是律師,」她說。

2. "What will I do?" he asked. 「我要做什麼?」他問。

3. "What a pretty girl she is!" he thought. 「她是多麼美麗的女孩子啊!」他想。

⑶如果引述動詞在句子中間, 亦即引述原句被 he said、she thought 等分開時, 引述的句子前半部之後用逗點, 後半部第一個字不大寫。例如:

"My father," she said, "is a lawyer." 「我的父親,」她說,「是律師。」

(4)引述一句以上時，所有句子均置於引號內。例如：

She said, "My father is a lawyer. He likes jogging." 她說：
「我父親是律師，他喜歡慢跑。」

27.3.　間接(引述)陳述句

直述原句為陳述句時，改變為間接引述有下列應注意的事項：
(1)如引述動詞為現在式，that 子句中之時式不變。that 也可以省略：

　1. He says, "I am a student." 他說：「我是學生。」

　　　間接引述：He *says* (that) he *is* a student. 他說他是學生。

　2. He says, "I am tired." 他說：「我累了。」

　　　間接引述：He *says* he *is* tired. 他說他累了。

但請注意：如引述兩個對等子句時，第二個 that 不省略。例如：

　3. He says, "I am tired and I am going to bed." 他說：「我累
　　　了，我要去睡覺了。」

　　　間接引述：He says he is tired and *that* he is going to bed.
　　　他說他累了，要去睡覺了。

(2)如引述動詞為過去式，間接引述之時式依下列原則改變：

直接引述　　──→	間接引述
簡單現在式	簡單過去式
現在進行式	過去進行式
現在完成式	過去完成式
現在完成進行式	過去完成進行式

簡單過去式	過去完成式
can/*will*/*shall*/*may* 等	*could*/*would*/*should*/*might* 等

例如：

1. He said, "I never drink tea." 他說：「我從不喝茶。」

   間接引述：He said (that) he never drank tea. 他說他從不喝茶。

2. "I am waiting for the bus." she said. 「我正在等公車。」她說。

   間接引述：She said (that) she was waiting for the bus. 她說（當時）她正在等公車。

3. She said, "I have done my homework." 她說：「我已經做完功課了。」

   間接引述：She *said* (that) she *had done* her homework. 她說她已經做完功課了。

4. He said, "I bought Mary a present." 他說：「我給 Mary 買了一份禮物。」

   間接引述：He *said* (that) he *had bought* Mary a present. 他說他給 Mary 買了一份禮物。

5. She said, "I can do it." 她說：「我能做這事。」

   間接引述：She said (that) she could do it. 她說她能做這事。

(3)引述動詞為過去式，在下列情形下，間接引述的子句中的時式可以不變：

(A)如引述子句中有明顯的時間用語，因此不會引起動作先後時間的混淆時，間接引述子句中的時式可不變。例如：

He *said*, "Tom *arrived* on Monday." 他說：「Tom 星期一到達了。」

間接引述: He *said* (that) Tom *arrived* on Monday. 他說 Tom 星期一到達了。(不必變成 had arrived)

(B)歷史事實之引述子句中, 時式不變。例如:

He said, "Confucius died in 479 B.C.." 他說:「孔子死於公元前 479 年。」

間接引述: He *said* that Confucius *died* in 479 B.C.. 他說孔子死於公元前 479 年。

(C)引述子句中之假設時式不變。例如:

The student *said*, "If I *tried* harder, I *might pass* the exam." 這學生說:「如果我更用功我可能會考試及格的。」

間接引述: The student *said* that if he *tried* harder he *might pass* the exam. 這學生說如果他更用功他可能會考試及格的。

(D)如引述動詞為過去式, 在間接引述子句中的 *might*、*should*、*would*、*used to* 等不變。例如:

She *said*, "They *should* be on time." 她說:「他們應該準時的。」

間接引述: She *said* that they *should* be on time. 她說他們應該準時的。

⑷間接引述子句中的「人稱」應適當地改變。例如:

He said, "*I* am a student." 他說:「我是學生。」

間接引述: *He* said that *he* was a student. 他說他是學生。

⑸其他的時間、方向、地方語詞，按以下方式改變。

直接引述	———→	間接引述

直接引述	間接引述
this　這	that　那
these　這些	those　那些
here　這兒	there　那兒
today　今天	that day　那天/當天
yesterday　昨天	the day before/the previous day　前一天
tomorrow　明天	the next day/the following day　第二天
the day before yesterday 前天	two days before　兩天前
the day after tomorrow 後天	in two day's time　兩天後
last night　昨晚	the night before/the previous night　前一天晚上
...ago　…之前 (如 a year ago)	...before　…之前 (a year before)
last week(year 等)前一週(去年)	the previous week(year)前一週(去年)
next year(week 等)明年(下週)	the following year(week)明年(下週)

例如：

1. "I will go to the movies **tomorrow**," he said. 他說：「我明天會去看電影。」

間接引述: He said that he would go to the movies *the next day*. 他說他第二天會去看電影。

2. She said, "I saw *this* man *a week ago*." 她說:「我一星期以前看過這個男人。」

間接引述: She said that she saw/had seen *that* man *a week before*. 她說她一星期以前看過那個男人。

27.4. 間接(引述)問句

間接問句之引述動詞為 *ask* '問'、*wonder* '想知道', 其後接 *if/whether* 或 *wh* 語詞(如 what、when 等)所引導的引述子句。原句的問號改為句號。

⑴如引述之原句為 *yes-no* 問句, 引述動詞後面接 *if* 或 *whether*。例如:

1. "Do you want to go shopping?" she asked. 她問(我)說:「你想去買東西嗎?」

間接引述: She asked *if/whether* I wanted to go shopping. 她問我是否想去買東西。

2. He asked, "Did you see Tom?" 他問(我)說:「你見到 Tom 嗎?」

間接引述: He asked(me) *if/whether* I had seen Tom. 他問我有沒有看見 Tom。

注意: (間接受詞[亦即被問者 me], 也可以加在引述動詞 *ask* 後面)。

(2)如引述之原句爲 **wh** 問句，引述動詞後面用原來的 **wh**—疑問詞。例如：

He asked, "What do you want?" 他問(我)說：「你想要什麼?」
間接引述：He asked **what** I wanted. 他問我想要什麼。

(3)間接問句中的字序與陳述句相同，並不倒裝。試比較：

1. "**Did you see** Tom?" he asked
→ He asked if **I had seen** Tom.
2. He asked, "What **do you want**?"
→ He asked what **I wanted**.

27.5. 間接(引述)命令與請求

命令句(祈使句)及請求句的間接引述形式是：
表示命令/請求的動詞＋受詞＋不定詞
常用的表示命令的引述動詞有：**tell**'吩咐'、**order** '命令'、**forbid** '禁止'等。

常用的表示請求的引述動詞有：**ask** '請求'、**beg** '懇求'、**request** '請求'等。
例如：

1. He said, "Sit down." 他說：「坐下來。」
→ He **told me to sit** down. 他吩咐我坐下來。(命令句之主詞是 you，因此，間接引述時爲 **me**)
如原命令句中提及對話者，則間接引述時引述動詞的受詞爲該對話者。
例如：

2. He said, "Sit down, Larry." 他說:「Larry，坐下來。」

→ He **told Larry to sit** down. 他吩咐 Larry 坐下來。

3. She said, "Could you help me?" 她說:「你可以幫助我嗎?」

→ She **asked me** to help her. 她請求我幫助她。

27.6. 間接(引述)建議

間接引述建議句時，通常用 **suggest + that** 子句或 **suggest + V-ing**。例如:

1. He said, "Let's go there by taxi." 他說:「我們坐計程車去那兒吧!」

→ He **suggested going** there by taxi.

或 He **suggested** that **we go** there by taxi. 他建議坐計程車到那兒去。

2. She said, "Why don't you open the door?" 她說:「你把門打開吧。」

→ She **suggested me opening** the door.

或 She **suggested that I open** the door.

《習題 31》

(A)將以下各句改爲間接引述陳述句。

例: He said, "I have some money."

→ *He said that he had some money.*

1. He said, "I have to do my homework."
2. David said, "I didn't say anything."
3. She says, "I am a nurse."
4. "My wife has just finished writing a book," he said.
5. "I am waiting for my husband," said the woman.
6. She said, "I would like to see Harry."
7. Ann said, "I will try my best."
8. Alice said, "I'll do it tomorrow."
9. Larry said, "I saw Tom last night."
10. They said, "We'll go next week."

(B)將下列各句改爲間接引述問句。

　　例： He asked, "Are you tired?"

　　　　 → *He asked if/whether I was tired.*

1. He asked, "Are you a student?"
2. She asked, "Did Larry buy this house?"
3. She asked, "Were you nervous?"
4. "Would you like to sit down?" he asked.
5. "What are you doing here?" she asked.
6. "When did he buy this car?" she asked.
7. "Where have you been?" she asked.
8. "Will you go downtown tomorrow?" he asked.

(C)將以下各句改爲間接引述命令句或請求句。

　　例： He said, "Sit down."

　　　　 → *He told me to sit down.*

　　　　 He said, "Could you sit down?"

→ *He asked me to sit down.*

1. She said to me, "Open the door."

2. The man said, "Don't let him go out."

3. "Let Tom come in," he said to me.

4. He said, "Put your things in this bag."

5. She said, "Would you stay for a few minutes?"

6. She said, "Could you tell me your name?"

7. I said to Tom, "Don't argue with your mother?"

8. She said, "Could you please turn on the radio?"

(D)將以下各句改為間接建議句。

例： "Let's go home," he said.

→ *He suggested that we go home.*

或 *He suggested our going home.*

1. "Let's sit down," he said.

2. "Let's go there by bus," he said.

3. "Let's go at once," she said.

4. Ann said, "Let's go to church."

5. Tom said, "Let's stand up."

6. Alice said, "Let's sing a song for Larry."

第二十八章
連接兩句簡單句時語詞之省略

28.1. 句中共有語詞的省略

當兩個簡單句表示「同意」或「不同意」時, 如用 *and*、*but* 等對等連接詞連接, 兩句所共有的相同語詞, 常以適當的方式省略, 以避免重複。這些省略法有以下幾種。

28.2. 連接兩句表示同意的簡單句

⑴兩句肯定句

㈠肯定句＋*and*＋第二句主詞＋動詞＋*too*

例如:

    1. I am a student. ⎫
       She is a student. ⎬→

    I am a student, ***and she is*** too. 我是學生, 她也是。

2. He likes English. ⎫
   She likes English. ⎬ →

He likes English, **and she does** too. 他喜歡英文，她也喜歡。

3. I will go tomorrow. ⎫
   They will go tomorrow. ⎬ →

I will go tomorrow, **and she will** too. 我明天會去，她也會。

從上面例句中，我們可注意到下列幾點：

(a)動詞為 *be* 時，第二句之動詞仍用 *be*。（如例句1）

(b)動詞為普通動詞時，第二句用適當的 *do* 動詞。（如例句2）

(c)動詞為含有助動詞的動詞組時，第二句仍用相同的助動詞。（如例句3）

(d)除動詞與主詞以外，第二句中與第一句相同的語詞省略。

這四點在以下各種句式中都適用。

(B)肯定句＋*and*＋*so*＋動詞＋第二句主詞

例如：

1. I am a student. ⎫
   She is a student. ⎬ →

I am a student, **and so is she**. 我是學生，她也是。

2. I like English. ⎫
   She likes English. ⎬ →

I like English, **and so does she**. 我喜歡英文，她也喜歡英文。

3. I can swim. ⎫
   They can swim. ⎬ →

I can swim, **and so can they**. 我會游泳，他們也會。

⑵兩句否定句

㈠否定句＋*and*＋第二句主詞＋動詞＋*not*＋*either*

例如：

1. I am not a student.
   She is not a student. } →

   I am not a student, *and she isn't either.* 我不是學生，她也不是。

2. I don't like Eaglish.
   She doesn't like English. } →

   I don't like English, *and she doesn't either.* 我不喜歡英文，她也不喜歡。

3. I haven't seen Tom for a long time.
   Jenny hasn't seen Tom for a long time. } →

   I haven't seen Tom for a long time, *and Jenny hasn't either.* 我很久沒看到 Tom 了，Jenny 也很久沒看到 Tom。

㈡否定句＋*and*＋*neither*＋肯定動詞＋第二句主詞

例如：

1. I am not a student.
   She is not a student. } →

   I am not a student, *and neither is she.* 我不是學生，她也不是。

2. I didn't see the movie.
   They didn't see the movie. } →

   I didn't see the movie, *and neither did they.* 我沒看這電

影，他們也沒看。

3. I won't help you.
   He won't help you. $\Big\}\rightarrow$

   I won't help you, **_and neither will he._** 我不會幫你，他也不會。

28.3. 連接兩句表示不同意或反義的簡單句

(A)肯定句＋*but*＋否定句主詞＋動詞＋*not*

例如：

1. I was tired.
   She wasn't tired. $\Big\}\rightarrow$

   I was tired **_but she wasn't._** 我累了，但她不累。

2. I saw her yesterday.
   He didn't see her yesterday. $\Big\}\rightarrow$

   I saw her yesterday, **_but he didn't._** 我昨天看見她，但是他沒有看見她。

3. I can swim.
   She can't swim. $\Big\}\rightarrow$

   I can swim, **_but she can't._** 我會游泳，但是她不會。

(B)否定句＋*but*＋肯定句主詞＋動詞

例如：

1. I am not a student.
   She is a student. $\Big\}\rightarrow$

I am not a student **but she is.** 我不是學生，但她是。

2. They don't like jogging.　} →
I like jogging.

They don't like jogging **but I do.** 他們不喜歡慢跑，但是我喜歡。

3. We won't go tomorrow.　} →
They will go tomorrow.

We won't go tomorrow, **but they will.** 我們明天不會去，但他們會。

《習題 32》

(A)將以下各對肯定句用「and...too」以及「and so＋動詞＋主詞」方式合併成一句。

例：He is a student.　} →
　　She is a student.

(a) *He is a student, and she is too.*

(b) *He is a student, and so is she.*

1. He was nervous.　} →
She was nervous.

2. He went there yesterday.　} →
She went there yesterday.

3. I like swimming.　} →
They like swimming.

4. Tom can swim.　} →
Mary can swim.

5. Ed is standing over there.
　Jane is standing over there. } →

(B)將以下各對否定句以「and...not...either」以及「and neither＋動詞＋主詞」方式
　合併為一句。

　例: He isn't a student.
　　　She isn't a student. } →

　　　He isn't a student and she isn't either.
　　　He isn't a student and neither is she.

1. I don't knon him.
　She doesn't know him. } →

2. He wasn't nervous.
　She wasn't nervous. } →

3. They didn't see me.
　He didn't see me. } →

4. I don't like swimming.
　She doesn't like swimming. } →

5. He shouldn't be late.
　I shouldn't be late. } →

(C)將以下各對句子用 but 連接成一句。

　例: He like apples.
　　　She doesn't like apples. } →

　　　He likes apples, but she doesn't.

1. I know Alice.
　He doesn't know Alice. } →

2. Jane likes lemon juice.
   We don't like lemon juice. } →

3. We don't have a car.
   Peter has a car. } →

4. I can't swim.
   Larry can swim. } →

5. They didn't understand me.
   He understood me. } →

English Grammar Juncture

英文文法階梯

康雅蘭 嚴雅貞 編著

專為想要重新學好文法的讀者所編寫的初級文法教材

- 一網打盡高中職各家版本英文課程所要求的文法基礎，為往後的英語學習打下良好基礎。

- 盡量以句型呈現文法，避免冗長解說，配上簡單易懂的例句，讓學習者在最短時間內掌握重點，建立整體架構。

- 除高中職學生外，也適合讓想要重新自修英文文法的讀者溫故知新之用。

Practical English Grammar

實用英文文法（完整版）

馬洵 劉紅英 郭立穎　編著
龔慧懿　編審

專為大專學生及在職人士學習英語所編寫的實用文法教材

- 涵蓋英文文法、詞彙分類、句子結構及常用句型。
- 凸顯實用英文文法，定義力求簡明扼要，以圖表條列方式歸納文法重點，概念一目了然。
- 搭配大量例句，情境兼具普遍與專業性，中文翻譯對照，方便自我進修學習。

實用英文文法實戰題本

馬洵 劉紅英　編著

- 完全依據《實用英文文法》出題，實際活用文法概念。
- 試題數量充足，題型涵蓋廣泛，內容符合不同程度讀者需求。
- 除每章的練習題外，另有九回綜合複習試題，加強學習效果。
- 搭配詳盡試題解析本，即時釐清文法學習要點。

Cloze & Writing Practice

克漏字與寫作練習（全新改版）

李文玲　編著

考場克敵制勝，教您「寫」脈賁張！
克漏字與寫作的完美組合，橫掃大小考試的終極利器！
30篇克漏字短文精心設計：
Basic 18篇─指導基礎句型寫作
Advanced 12篇─傳授進階作文技巧

You Can Write!

寫作導引（全新改版）

李文玲　編著

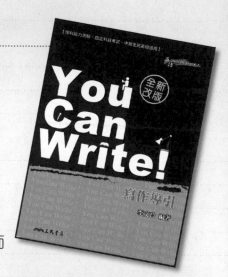

大家一起來「寫」拼
1. 從寫作概念的介紹到各種文體的寫作策略，循序漸進。
2. 近百題的實戰演練。
3. 每章另闢小單元，分享寫作的小技巧與常面臨的問題。